N O

O R D I N A R Y

S T A R

A soldier is summoned to the North Pole, days before the year changes, told to fix the great Clock for a celebration. He has no idea what to do.
A girl, hunted for the crime of being born, almost dies out on the ice. She is rescued by the last polar bear left alive.
A library waits for them both, a library built over a span of a hundred years, forgotten in the basement of an ice shack.
The world hasn't known hunger or sickness in hundreds of years. It has also forgotten love and beauty.
The year is 2524.

Inspired by the short stories of Ray Bradbury, this futuristic young adult novel is set in a world where Christmas -among other things- is obsolete and a Clock is what keeps the fragile balance of peace.

Written in three installments, this is the breathtaking and sensual story of how two unlikely people change the world, and each other, one book at a time.

Also by M.C. Frank

Ruined
a Jane Eyre Regency retelling

NO ORDINARY STAR

PART 1

M . C .   F R A N K

Title: No Ordinary Star – Part One
Author: M. C. Frank

This book is a work of fiction. All names, characters, places and incidents are products of the author's imagination or are used fictitiously and are not to be construed as real. Any resemblance to actual events, locales, organizations, or persons living or dead, is entirely coincidental.

Inspired by the short stories of Ray Bradbury

and

dedicated to the person who taught me to love them.

In the end, you didn't make me hate the sun*. On the night that you left there was a full moon.
I haven't looked at it since.

*Reference to a short story by Ray Bradbury,
'The Rocket Man'
from *'The Illustrated Man'*

THE DESERT IS scorching hot outside his goggles. The soldier shoots an uneasy glance over his shoulder, to the rest of his squad. His fellow officers are walking briskly in a mostly straight line, boots sinking in the soft sand, cheeks tanned by the scorching sun.

The one walking in front of him lifts a hand to wipe the sweat from his brow, and the soldier smirks. His highly evolved skin-sculpt goggles prevent sweat, sand and dirt from landing on his eyes and obscuring his vision, making it easier to see.

Or at least they were, up until a few minutes ago.

A few minutes ago, a message cue popped up on his visor. He can see it in front of him now, as he trudges onto the next dune, blinking in the corner of his left eye, driving him crazy.

He can't open it for a quite a few hours yet; he won't take a break until tomorrow. They are only allowed a single one-hour break per day, and to do something like pause in the middle of a drill in the Morocco desert to open a message that's waiting on your personal net, well... Cadets have been court-martialed for less -everyone knows that.

This soldier knows it better than most.

He's the brightest, the best of the bunch, some say. Some others say he's just the most obedient, the one less expected to deviate from the rules, that's all there is to his success in the regiment. The truth is much simpler: he's just the best at everything.

The soldier thinks that without conceit; it's just a fact, written in his DNA.

"Ten seconds," someone growls from the front. They're supposed to walk a distance of two miles in under fifteen minutes. The soldier is almost done in nine and a half.

He lifts his long legs, hardly breaking a sweat, and pushes forward, quickly overtaking everyone but his General. His thigh muscles feel tense from the exercise and their familiar ache as they stretch numbs his mind pleasantly. A lock of white-blond hair flops to his forehead, and he lifts a gloved hand to push it back. His vision is clear for miles, the sky a sickening blue, the brown sand going on forever. The message cue interrupts the thin clouds, coming in and out of his vision maddeningly.

This is getting boring. When are they going to

start some real training? The others are more than ten steps behind.

"Good job, lieutenant," the General says to him as soon as the rest of the officers line up, snapping to attention.

The soldier -who is really a lieutenant- stands absolutely still, not nodding, not blinking, not acknowledging the General's praise in any way. He disciplines his long body to stay silent, not a muscle twitching, not one breath out of order. His eyes look straight ahead. He knows that's the kind of posture that will impress his General the most, after a tough drill like that.

What won't impress him is how itchy his fingers are getting from wanting to open the message on his goggles. Just five more hours until free time, the soldier thinks. Then you can delete it.

one

Three hours earlier, in quite another part of the world, the old man everyone calls 'the Clockmaster' drags his feet to the green door of his shack and opens it with difficulty. There's fresh snow behind it, weighing it down, and beads of sweat gather on his wrinkled brow, falling onto his white beard, as he pushes with all his strength into the steel and wood until it gives way. He closes the door behind him, locking it carefully, as he's done every morning for the past fifteen years or so.

The sky is a dazzling painting of blues and reds and grays -it takes his breath away. The day is crisp and clear, almost like every other morning he's taken the same walk in the snow, hiking to the forest and back.

Today is a bit different, though.

He has a feeling of finality at the pit of his stomach, as though every step he takes is changing the world. Old age is finally catching up with you, old timer, he thinks. Crystal snowflakes twirl about him, landing on his red cheeks. Every step lifts a cloud of them around his black, heavy boots as he walks towards the dim outline of the fir trees.

It will be Christmas in a week.

Not that anyone will notice.

You've lived alone for too long, old man, and you're beginning to imagine things. Christmas! What a thing to remember at times like these.

He thinks of the huge hollow disc that has to be filled strategically with cogwheels and gears, standing in the middle of his cold little room, but he hasn't been able to concentrate on his work for days.

The new year simply won't dawn if his Clock isn't ready to chime it in. He stops, breathless, lifting his eyes to the skies, and chuckles softly to himself. *Will the truth ever be known?*

Probably not.

So you say there is no Father Christmas
You say there is no Santa Claus
Reindeer cannot fly, it's all a grown-up lie...

It's a song older than time itself -older even than him; what made it suddenly pop into his head?

He murmurs it, prodding himself to keep walking in time with the melody. He doesn't remember all the words, but the music is sad and nostalgic; it reminds him of a home long gone and sunny days filled with love and the smell of cinnamon. The love lives on.

So you say there is no Father Christmas

The Clockmaster walks on, burying his chin in the thick, fur lapels of his coat. His steps feel heavier today. His large, white head feels light, as though a mere gust of wind could blow it away like a bird. Like the icy powder that drifts from the sky to land on his collar.

He sees the sniper a split second before he shoots.

There's a deafening sound, and the next minute a sharp pain blossoms in his chest, and he feels himself falling away from sight, sinking into the snow, its crystals parting to welcome his weight.

It takes him a moment to realize that he's no longer moving. He tries to find his bearings, and buries his sturdy staff into the ground, pushing his weight on its hand-crafted handle so that he can stand, but he falls back on trembling limbs.

The sniper is gone; the Clockmaster he didn't even have time to see if he was a member of the Guard or a free-shooter. He just appeared out of nowhere, a black silhouette somewhere behind the trees, and shot him. He surely was an easy target, walking in plain sight out in the open, a dark spot in stark contrast to the glowing twilight reflected off the bluish snow.

The pain is numbing but his mind is falling asleep with the cold, too. Something is gnawing at him, a mere sliver of a thought at the edges of his consciousness. What is it?

"So you say there is no Father Christmas..." No it's not that. "Twenty-five twenty-five," he mutters.

Two numbers, identical; they remind him of something, but he can't quite grasp what that is. The numbers hover on the fringes of his tired memory, and still their meaning eludes him. So much information, so many experiences, all of them ticking away like minutes on one of his cuckoo clocks; wars, kisses, celebrations, changes, pain. All of it gone now.

Soon it will be gone forever. Irrevocably.

"Twenty-five twenty-five."

People used to think he was something like a timekeeper, or at the very least, a memory-keeper. But these memories he's collected so meticulously over the years -they have been his own personal demons as well.

It's certainly not his job to keep them -it shouldn't be anybody's job.

He's just another human being.

And he hasn't been exceptionally good at that, either.

He used to hope that he would be able to pass the flame on to someone else, someone more worthy, more clever and compassionate, but as the cold travels to his extremities, he starts to think he may have no time for that. He wasted all his years, and now it's too late.

"Constantine," he whispers, and a lone tear freezes on his cheek. "Twenty-five, twenty-five. Felix, my hope."

Now he remembers, if just for a second.

It takes less than a minute for the falling snow to cover him like a shroud.

He falls asleep looking at the stars.

And in his dreams comes a fairy, riding an angel clouded in plush white fur, her hair on fire. She looks down on him from atop her perch on the angel's back.

He feels a smile creeping across his frozen face as her huge brown eyes fill his vision. He hears - in his dream, always- steps crunching on the snow beside him, he feels a warm, trembling hand gently touch his icy grave.

"Father...?" the fairy says, and he is convinced he's dreaming, if he ever had a doubt, for this is a word he hasn't heard in years. "Father Christmas?"

He wants to tell her that's not his name, it was just a song of the Old Ones he was singing, but in the dream his lips are sealed shut and little icicles have begun to drift on his stiff white beard.

"It should have been me," the fairy says in a trembling voice that sounds like a whispered bell. She starts to weep soundlessly.

If he could speak, he'd warn her about the sniper, he'd yell at her to run. If he could speak, he'd whisper to her the number one more time; maybe she could help avoid disaster.

But he can't, and so the fairy just sits there beside him, her dirty, torn dress pooling around her on the grey snow, holding his hand and sobbing, in plain sight. There might still be snipers surrounding the plain, eyes peeking behind the snow-capped trees, but she doesn't move. She holds his cold hand in her bare ones until his breathing gets even.

Until her beautiful dark eyes are the only thing he remembers from this broken, frozen world.

t w o

The world falls to pieces with a loud crash a few minutes later. Or maybe it is a few days later, or a few years; it's all the same for the Clockmaster, who's still lying in the ice.

The fairy is still crying three days later, crying for a life lost in vain, crying for the things the old man didn't say as his life was spilled on the snow, soaking her dress red. She's not a fairy, not really. She's just a girl, small boned and wild-haired.

She's a crying girl, a hunted girl. She's a girl who's about to become a dead girl. But suddenly, on the third day after the Clockmaster's death, the girl's crying turns to screams. There's a harsh, breaking sound slicing the silence first, then a small splash. Then ice floating in a hole.

That's when the screams start. At first they're awful, blood-curling, sharp sounds that make the trees around the old man's resting place shudder -even though by now she's left it far behind- and the stars break to a million pieces.

The fairy -who isn't a fairy- screams and screams and the angel -who, in fact, is something else entirely- takes off towards the horizon. Her screams escalate until they're unbearable. But there's no one to hear them.

Even the snipers have gone days ago, mistakenly thinking their job done when they killed the old man instead of the girl -they didn't think for a minute there would be anybody else out in the vast whiteness, anybody but their prey. The girl screams with all she's got one last time.

Then, silence.

three

It's the shortest day of the year tonight. The Arctic is white, as it's always been, an expanse of icy desert sprinkled with a few clusters of fir trees, star-studded heavens purple with night overhead.

This part of the world used to be called 'Alaska' or some such exotic name when there were people here, but it's been years since human eyes have seen the breathtaking cold beauty of these lands. Traditions of candy-stripe-wrapped presents and a big, fat man who always wore red toiling among his pointy-eared helpers have long since ceased to exist, along with the civilizations which created them.

Change is a good thing, people have always said -and they still do, now, in the dawning of another year of the twenty-sixth century- and so they continue to improve themselves and their lives, driven by that elusive ambition to surpass each other and their own, degrading human needs. Which they have achieved, for the most part.

There is no hunger in the world, no illness, no discomfort. No discord. It's simply been eliminated. How could the human race, after conquering the lengths of the Solar System, after perfecting the science of the body and the brain, after, in short, outgrowing its own strengths and amazing its own intelligence time and again; how could it fail to eliminate its own weaknesses? It has not. Everything is perfect, which in the case of the vast Arctic land, translates to quiet. Empty.

No need for towns up here, exposed to the cold and darkness and solar winds, so all that's left is a few Power Towers and the Intergalactic Space Station.

And the Clockmaster's ice shack.

It's not really a 'shack', Felix thinks as he leans back on the swirly-patterned comforter on the low-back titanium sofa. On the inside it's pretty much like any of the luxurious apartments piled on top of each other in the home where he grew up with four other children, in New Baghdad, in the European East. He's seen pictures of how it looks on the outside, but he hasn't been outside the door.

He imagines it as a sort of wooden structure like the one he's seen in Visuals and Projections of fairytales from the Old World, half covered in thick eternal snow that never melts, its tin roof the only splotch of color in the endless white.

Truth be told, he couldn't care less.

He's been in this godforsaken place for more than two days now and he's got nothing to show for it. It's starting to get on his nerves.

The place smells of wood and fresh snow, and he's not used to things smelling quite so much. His tiny cubicle at school is sterilized, as is every public place. There's also a lot of unnecessary objects around, and he's tired of feeling so cluttered and seeing so much color all the time. There's even a bed in the second room -whoever heard of a home having a second room? But the shack is huge, three rooms in all, one filled with Old World electronics he has no idea how to work, as well as a wooden table, and one with an old-fashioned bed and a tilted roof which gives him a headache every time he looks at it.

He's spent all of his time so far in this third room, which has only this sofa, the Pod and the Projector, covering a wall from the floor to the ceiling. The standard bathroom cubicle is tucked out of sight in the far-left corner. If he keeps his eyes trained away from the little windows with the frilly red curtains and the huge green door, he can almost concentrate.

He's concentrating right now on his hunger.

He's only got two pills left -he didn't think to take provisions with him-, and he intends to ration them for as long as he can; hopefully he won't have to stay much longer here, and he can go back before he gets to actually starving. Not that he's done anything constructive so far. He's got half a mind to get in the Transport Pod right now and get back to school, where his professors are already wondering what has happened to their star lieutenant.

He heard it on the news last night. It was a live Projection from the Terrestrial Channel, dubbing him 'the lost prince'. They played it three times during the entire day. Every time it came on, he smirked, thinking that he'd been missing barely two days. He knows, of course, that the Counsil takes very seriously every facility that uses the Planet's funds, and a military school even more so, and so it was only a matter of hours before he was missed at the half-day head count and hell was raised.

He's been 'the prince' of The New Baghdad Training Military School ever since he aced every test in the try-outs for advanced military positions and made lieutenant just two months ago. His comrades started calling him 'the prince' and joke that he was having a much easier time of it, but they all knew that wasn't true. There were times that he didn't think he would make it to the next brutal level of training -still, he's survived.

Until now.

The Clockmaster's message arrived almost two days ago now. He let it blink in a corner on the visor of his goggles, intending to watch it in the one free hour between three and four in the morning.

The world has had no sleep in half a century.

There's no need. It's always light inside, and the human body can get whatever it needs in a capsule. It gets its food from a red and brown one three times a day, its rest and health maintenance every morning from the green striped Health Discs. So there you have it. One more problem eliminated.

In military school, of course, you need to rest your brain a little from all the yelling and intense exercising and the electrode-transmitted orders that enter your system from the nerve endings on your skin.

So you can walk into the Transport Pod and go for a swim in a beach in Santa Mauricia, in the Tropics. Or maybe pop out for a quick stroll through the stars in one of the daily Shuttles. You can go visit the Virtual Data Bases in Cairo, or you can lay on the floor staring at the narrow strip of ceiling that covers your tiny cubicle. Just as long as you're back in an hour for the head count.

So that's when Felix popped the Clockmaster's message in the Visual and turned the volume way down to listen to it without being overheard.

And that was the start of the end of the world.

Felix has never heard of anyone having a grandfather.

He's not even sure what a grandfather is.

Felix, just like pretty much every child born after the Second Enlightenment, hasn't grown up in a family. He simply doesn't have one. His characteristics, his high IQ, his height and even his personality, they have all been elected by the ES, the Elimination System, which is pretty much the greatest achievement of the twenty-sixth century. Yes, it's true. Humanity has finally been able to take control of the race, the intelligence and the skills of its own population, and there is no need to leave it at chance: people are created in tubes, not hospitals. They are bred in homes in the care of specifically trained people, and they end up becoming the improved human race man has dreamt of since the dawn of time.

This is pretty much what the Second Enlightenment was all about.

And now, Chairman Kun, a genius of his age, has perfected the system of rebuilding the Planet from its very cradle, with the Revision. People are intentionally created, instead of just happening to be born.

Imperfections are almost eliminated -the Elimination System was created for just this purpose. And it's worked wonders both in the Planet and the Colonies. To think, people didn't used to live more than eighty, perhaps a hundred years. And now it's very much expected that no human being will have a reason to expire before their three-hundredth year. Mankind is well on its way to becoming immortal.

Felix grew up in a home with four other children and a woman named Mother Alex. She isn't their mother, of course, no one is, but she was kind and clean and didn't beat them.

Felix was the oldest when he came into the house -eight years old.

It was winter solstice that day, too.

"Are you from the Colonies?" a three-year-old boy, Karim, had asked him.

"Do I *look* like I'm from the Colonies?" Felix had retorted, angrily. He still had a hard time looking anyone in the face, even if that anyone was a little brown boy chewing on his thumb.

"Your hair ith white," Karim had persisted, drool dripping from his lower lip.

Now he's one of his best friends, as well as his right hand torchbearer. He joined the Military three years after Felix.

"It's not white, it's yellow," Felix had pressed his lips together. "Will you go ask the lady to wipe your face?"

He knew well enough that he looked different than anyone else in the house. The other two boys, older than him, had called him 'a timer freak' (meaning an Old Timer, only he didn't know all the slang back then) and had pushed him into the Pod, sending him off to a desert on Mars the first day. He'd had a hell of a time working the Pod to get back again, but he managed it. And he didn't tell the lady who everyone called 'Mother'.

He'd already managed to survive eight years of his life in the highest-security prison on the Planet, he wasn't about to start asking for help now.

"Tho where'd you come from?" Karim persisted, beginning to suck his other thumb.

"Don't you have any lessons to learn?"

Felix was busy with a Visual that promised it would teach him how to write in ten days maximum, but had so far refused to even start, since Felix hadn't worked one of the stupid things before.

"You hafta press your palm on it and then scan your eye," Karim said, proceeding to press his wet little hand on top of his, and moving their joined hands in front of the screen.

Felix felt a jolt of electricity run through him at the little boy's touch.

He hadn't been touched in eight years -his entire life, actually. "All right, all right, I've got it," he said quickly, pushing the baby away.

It was there and then he decided to do whatever it took to get his hands on a pair of Hydro gloves that became one with your hand, just like the ones the Guards who escorted him from his cell wore. He received his own pair a few years later, when he passed his first Military test. He hasn't taken them off since then.

"You a bad boy?" Karim asked, his voice trembling a little.

Felix sighed and turned to look at him. The boy's eyes, like two shiny black beads, were filling with tears.

"Don't tell the others, ok?" he said to Karim. "Promise?"

Karim nodded furiously. "Or the Cailman can eat my heart."

Felix felt a sharp sound escape his lips. The boys turned from the other wall, where they'd been absorbed in their routine Visual tests on two identical screens, and stared at him as he roared with laughter. This shrieking sound coming from his lips was new as well. He didn't care for it either.

"Don't say things like that," he said seriously to the baby. "It takes less than that to stick you in the Box."

Karim's eyes widened.

Everyone knew what the 'Box' was. It was the high security prison, the biggest one in the Planet. No one came alive out of it -since their crimes were so great as to be a serious danger to humanity. Chairman Kun takes dangers to humanity very seriously indeed.

"You from the Box?" Karim said, taking a shaky step back, his little legs stumbling over the diaper 'Mother' had quickly slapped on underneath his Hydro pants.

Everyone was dressed in this grey, elastic material that kept you warm and safe, Felix had quickly discovered. At first he was missing his cotton pants and filthy shirt, but he was already getting used to the luxury of neither freezing nor being hot or dirty or prickly. Hydro didn't allow dirt particles to latch onto it, plus, as he learned later, it adjusted to his body temperature. Hydro was good, he liked it.

"Yep," he said, leaning down to stare into Karim's black eyes with his intense, blue ones. He opened them wide, trying to look as foreign and scary as possible. "And you know why they stuck me in there? I ate a dirty baby, that's why."

Karim started screaming and ran for 'Mother', who was currently taking a break in the waters of Indonesia. She wasn't, that was a lie, but Felix didn't know then what a 'Mother' was, so how could he know she was being recharged, her programming checked and her settings updated for the month? He didn't. He didn't know a lot of things -still doesn't.

One of the elder boys took off his earplugs and threatened to throw Karim out the window -they were on the fiftieth floor- and thankfully *that* shut him up.

Five days later Felix was allowed his first break, and he went straight to the Arctic, to the Perennial Site. It was nothing but ice on a lake yet, but he could already see the Terrestrial trains arriving in the distance from inside the Pod's glass. He reached out absent-mindedly to push the button and get out, but his hands touched something warm and hairy.

He looked down. Karim's beady eyes were gleaming hopefully up at him.

That was the first time Felix cursed in the world outside the Box. "What the timers are you doing here?"

Karim's eyes were already misting. "Why did you want to come here?" he asked, stubbornly, ignoring Felix's question. "You keep asking for an invitation for the Pernerniry, but only richies are invited."

"It's the Perennial," Felix said, "and you're not supposed to transport until you're at least six, or you could die. Or stay like a dwarf forever. You're going back."

He started pressing the buttons. He'd learned how to work the Pod *and* write within five days instead of ten.

"Nooooo!" Karim wailed, looking as though his heart was breaking. "Pleeeeeease let me stay. I want to see the Clockster."

Felix felt himself grow hot underneath his

Hydro suit. Immediately it began to cool him down, and dry his sweat, but he didn't feel any better inside, where it mattered. "It's the Clockmaster," he said quietly to Karim, opening the door and stepping out into the cold, while Karim grabbed on to his knee, scared of the strange sleek surface his little shoes where slipping on the ice. "And he's the reason I'm out of the Box."

four

tin soldier

That was the first and only time he's been in the cold climate. All his training has taken place in the Tropics or the Ecuador since he joined the Military, but he's always wearing a full head-gear these days, so he hasn't felt the poisonous earth air on his face since he was eight years old. Some say it's not really poisonous, but Felix isn't taking any chances.

He kept hoping for an invite to the Perennial Celebration, hoping to watch the Clockmaster ringing in the New Year, even from afar, but of course it never happened. Every year, shortly after the Solstice, the Pods to the Arctic close, because the Site is being prepared for the greatest celebration in the Planet.

A huge stadium is built on Site, huge enough to hold hundreds of thousands of spectators, and in the middle a stage, visible by all, where the Clockmaster sets his new Clock to tick the last minute of the old year away.

Then they all cheer and Chairman Kun

addresses them, his message broadcasted to every corner of the Planet and the Colonies via the Terrestrial Channel, and that's it. The party starts in the first moments of the New Year and lasts for a whole fortnight. After that fortnight, the Elite of the Planet, which basically means the caste of educated, wealthy officials, genetic engineers and Counsil members, as well as the thousands of other middle-class guests that were lucky enough to have been invited, go back to their homes to rest and be restored to their pre-alcohol-drinking, shouting-and-dancing and arctic-air-breathing healthy states.

It's rumored that some of the most eccentric Elites have begun to bring some kind of actual food to the Celebration, illegally of course, and much less poisonous than the timers' disgusting concoctions. But still, the guests gorge themselves on forbidden fruits and liquids, and reach home in a state almost near sickness, from which no pill could bring them back, so many of them have to be transported to a Health Spot immediately. How embarrassing.

Felix has no idea why all these incandescently rich people wish to degrade themselves by engaging in these Old Time customs.

As for the Clockmaster, well, that's a different story.

He's a legend.

Some people say he's some sort of time-keeper,

or a wizard, like the tales of the Old World describe.

What he is to Felix is his savior.

He was to be executed on the day he turned nine, which was about a month after the solstice. Instead, he was let go. Just like that. For no obvious reason.

Felix hasn't heard of it ever happening on the Planet. Of course, one could argue that he'd been imprisoned just like that, for no obvious reason as well, but he has the uneasy feeling that he's done a crime bigger than Jupiter and he just can't remember it because he was either too young, or he's blocked it out.

He's sure he was a threat to humanity, and he's been very careful not to do anything that might hurt the Planet or the Chairman again. He's always been the first to obey any order, without question, the first to volunteer in the most risky operations, the first to log in for the head count. He hasn't ever followed Karim or his other friends when they invited him to an obscure opium-maker's den in Saturn 3.14 -not that it actually existed when they got there, the owner had moved it to the Western Regions, which are still not safely atmosphere-regulated, but why risk it?

He'll never forget where he began and where he's ended up, and he'll never stop being grateful to his rescuer. He's probably the most law-obedient citizen in the One World.

At least, he was until two days ago.

When the Visual arrived -the Vis, as they call them-, he finally saw the Clockmaster.

He was nothing like he had imagined him to be -if anything, he looked more like an Old Time wizard, like the rumors suggested.

Then he didn't have time to look anymore, because the old man was speaking.

He fingers the chip he transferred the Vis in before he left school, now in the pocket of his grey Hydro suit, which, among other things, keeps his body temperature level, and protects him from scratches. It's sculpted to his body, a tunic and a pair of fitted pants with a black line running down the length of his leg, which indicates him as Military. A row of buttons is concealed in the front, each one with its specific use, containing his pills and discs, but he's taken yesterday's and he wants to save the rest for later, so he doesn't need them for now.

He sighs.

"What on earth do you want from me, old man?" Felix mutters.

He can't help it; he's starting to get desperate.

He knows he owes a debt much larger than anyone can imagine to this man, and that's why for the first time in his seventeen years, he's broken the law for his sake.

But everything has been going the timer's way since he came here.

Bored out of his mind, he slips the chip in the Visual Projector.

So far, he's found nothing. He's pressed his gloved fingers to every surface of the old-fashioned metallic table, the few chairs and the Projector -the PR-, hoping he'd find something concealed somewhere, a clue, anything. There isn't a clock in sight, which worries him even more. The walls are bare too, except for the timer windows, right by the Transport Pod Portal, but as soon as he came, Felix pressed the button on the wall that flicks open the lights and the next one that shuts the blinds down, because he feels more comfortable in closed spaces.

He's been outside about ten times in his life, all in deserts and harsh mountaintops, part of his strict military training, and he hates the outdoors with a passion.

'Hello, my dear boy,' the Clockmaster's voice says from the PR.

The Projector is nothing more than an intelligent screen, made of paper-thin glass, and there are no buttons on it, although it is interactive once it's turned on. The PR screens come in all sizes and capacities, but this one is of the highest quality. For one thing, it's massive, covering the entire wall next to the green door, and for another it can get feeds from the Terrestrial Channel, but you can also load all sorts of net browsers and message chips on it. Generally, you can do anything via the PR, from contacting someone on the other end of the Planet on a live Vis, to browsing through the Planet's Common Database for un-restricted information.

Felix has no interest in any of that. He just sits back and gets ready to be confused again by the Clockmaster's message.

Now that he's gotten used to seeing it, his face looks a bit wrinkled but kind, his skin weathered, his blue eyes brilliant in contrast to the white halo of hair around his forehead. Felix's own eyes are the exact same color, his cheekbones pronounced, his hair a brilliant yellow, almost white.

Felix's mop of wheat-blond hair has a streak at the front dyed permanently black, as of last month when he made lieutenant. His left ear is pierced with a tiny stud which contains a locator chip. Everyone has one of these, usually right beneath the top layer of skin on their left forearm, but the Chairman's soldiers are pierced with an additional one, in case of a military emergency.

Felix watches the Clockmaster wet his lips with his tongue, and wonders if they will execute him for ripping it off.

Looking for a distraction, he pauses the Vis and traces the Clockmaster's jaw with a mental finger. He can see it, plain as day: they look the same.

The Clockmaster is not wearing goggles like Felix is, nor is he as tall and lean. He's got almost no muscles, and he looks as though the last Health Discs he took haven't worked properly. He's not wearing a Hydro suit, nor is he wearing his Clockmaster's official black cloak designed to remind the People of the Old World's tales. Instead he's wearing a soft, white garment, with two pointy things around the collar, and a row of buttons down the front, which look plastic and useless.

And yet, no one can deny it.

The brilliant blue eyes are the same, the facial expressions, the dimple in his left cheek as he opens his mouth to speak. Even the gesture he makes with his hand -Felix feels chills run down his spine at the thought of how many times he's made the exact same gesture when he's looking for the right words.

'If you're watching this, I'm dead,' the Clockmaster says somberly, his blue eyes crinkling with kindness under his bushy white eyebrows. 'I've scheduled this Visual to reach you, Felix, my precious boy, every morning for the past nine years, in case I don't return from one of my long walks in the snow.'

The Clockmaster smiles as though at a thought that transports him somewhere the Pods can't take you.

'It's so beautiful, the snow,' he goes on, and Felix wants to strangle him until he gets to the point, but he sits still, mesmerized by words that sound familiar, but he has no idea what they mean. *Beautiful. Snow. My precious boy.*

'I wish you had come here to grow up in this wonderful place, with someone who loves you, instead of...' the Clockmaster presses his lips together. 'It feeds your soul in a way no pill ever will,' he adds and there's a sadness in his eyes that makes Felix want to cry like Karim used to when he wouldn't take him in the Pod.

It feeds your soul. Someone who loves you. More foreign words.

'First things first, my boy,' the Clockmaster shakes himself out of his reverie and smiles. 'My name is Ulysses. And I am your grandfather.'

Felix swipes his fingers on the PR and the image freezes again.

Was the old man crazy? he wonders, not for the first time.

He suddenly doesn't have the heart to listen to any more. He knows it by heart anyway by now, much good it will do him.

'Now, listen carefully,' the Clockmaster - Ulysses- will say in a minute, his eyebrows pushing together. 'You're a smart boy and I'm sure I can trust you, if anyone in this forsaken planet is to be trusted.' Ulysses' voice will take on a bitter tinge here, and Felix, replaying it in his head for the twentieth time in two days, wonders again what that expression means.

He swipes his hand again, fast-forwarding it until he reaches the most important place in the Clockmaster's Vis.

'Tell no one that I'm gone. Get in the Pod *right now*, and transport to my ice shack in the Arctic, and finish my work before the day of the Perennial Celebration. You know what my work is, but I can't say anything else on here, in case it's leaked. Nothing is more important than this. Leave your work, your school, your position. Just get on a Pod and go. You'll find further instructions there. Now, I have loaded the coordinates on this Visual, so if you'll just load it on there, you'll be in the Arctic the next second, and once you-'

Felix freezes the PR.

He heard a strange sound coming from the general direction of the windows. He gets up, and stands still in the small room, unsure of what to do.

There are no unexpected sounds in his world - except for when he's on site for training, of course.

There are all sorts of sounds of exploding guns there, and what reaches his ears right now is nothing like that, but still he does what he'd do if he heard a Slayer .34 going off in the distance: he slams his head gear in place, checks his vitals, and grabs the Protector .44 that was strapped to his thigh. A Protector .44 is a smaller gun than the Slayer .34, but quieter and more deadly in smaller distances. It's the one thing the soldiers are required to carry on their suits at all times, whether they're off duty or not. He didn't expect to be stranded up here for so long, or he would have packed more gear. At least he has a gun with him.

The sound continues, a banging, scratching sound that's coming from outside, and he locates it at the green door. There's a key placed in the lock, and Felix looks at it uncertainly, but there's no other way out, so he decides to try his luck.

He struggles with the rusty hinges until the old-fashioned key has turned once, then twice, then three times, and then, just as the banging has started to shake the entire house, threatening to bring the door down, he swings it open.

And there, standing in front of him, glowing white as it's silhouetted against the dark, bluish sky, is a huge bear.

five

tin soldier

Felix Hunter is a Citizen of the Planet, recently a lieutenant of Chairman Kun's Intergalactic Armies, and a holder of one of the highest Intelligence Rates in the One World. He is almost eighteen years old. He has blue eyes and blond hair with a thick black lock falling on his forehead. He is six feet tall, and his heart beats exactly twenty times a minute.

He hasn't felt cold or pain; he hasn't known his parents or even spoken to a girl; and he hasn't once given the Chairman a cause to be ashamed of the new heights the One World has reached under his leadership.

Yet today, on the evening of the winter solstice of the year 2524, Felix Hunter will do all three.

First comes the cold.

As he opens the door, the bear lowers its paw, only it doesn't drop it to the ground. Felix feels the great weight of the animal's warm limb as it pushes on his arm, making him stagger. The animal is warm and its breath billows whitely in front of its face, as it lets out an agonized growl.

A cold wind is blowing cross the empty plains, howling eerily as it blows past him inside the door, but Felix's suit keeps him warm, and the goggles allow him to see for miles in the descending twilight, unhindered by the icy cold snowflakes that land on his hair.

Then he sees the trees.

He's seen them before, of course, in Reproductions and Instructional Visuals, he's even seen some up close in the Sichuan forest, where they took them for training two years ago in the part of Europea that used to be China.

But this is completely different. They're dark masses, looming in the distance, crowned by an expanse of exquisite purple sky, bursting with yellow, purple, pink and red. It's so beautiful and so bizarre that his eyes hurt. Sunset, that's what it is. He's never seen it happening right in front of his eyes -he has the strange sensation of feeling as though he's inside an Instructional Vis, but it's real, no Vis, the sun a big ball of fire sinking behind the trees, and the weird sensation is giving him whiplash.

He feels his mouth drop open and tries to wake up from the strange fascination of watching every little tuft of snowy grass, of trying to distinguish every spruce needle in the fir trees ahead or count the colors of the sky, but he has no time to concentrate on either. He's pushed violently from behind, and in his surprise, he stumbles and falls face-first into the snow.

He gets up immediately, cursing. "Timer beast," he mutters under his breath, pulling his Protector .44 and leveling it right between the bear's eyes.

He hesitates.

Now why would he do that? He's trained to shoot to kill without a moment's hesitation, and although most of his training has taken place in virtual holographic war sites, this shouldn't feel so different.

Except through his goggles he can discern the radius of different colors in the bear's irises, as it regards him somberly. He can smell the snow on its thick white fur, and the earth on its paws. He lowers his gun, feeling unsteady, as though he's suddenly been transported to one of the Colonies where it takes a moment to get used to the weightlessness of space. No, not even there. To another world.

He feels suddenly dizzy, and shakes his head to clear it, but he can't move very well with the goggles on. For the first time since putting them on, five years ago, he wishes he could go back to just seeing things with his weak, human eyes. But that's just stupid, isn't it?

The bear lets out a growl. Felix snaps his attention back to the white beast, and as though satisfied that it's got his attention, the bear puts its head down and starts running.

"Good riddance," Felix yells at it and makes for the door.

He lingers a moment, in spite of himself, and his long legs turn by themselves towards the trees, as though they itch to explore their hidden treasures. He takes one step and hears a low growl.

The bear is puffing right behind his elbow.

"What?" Felix screams in frustration. This isn't real. It can't be.

This kind of exotic animal has been extinct for years. He studied hard on ancient life-form species for his History exams, he even watched Visuals about the Old Times. How the timers has this beast survived up here? How has it escaped the Researchers? And why does it behave like one of the Army Dogs, who run back and forth when they've discovered a hidden uranium crypt or a dead body and they want you to follow them?

Oh.

Felix starts running. In a second the bear has overtaken him, its great paws kicking up a storm of powdery snow in Felix's face.

They run for about ten minutes like that, and although Felix has no trouble keeping the pace of the bear, his calve muscles are starting to burn from struggling against the deepening blanket of snow, and his breath comes in white puffs in front of his face. He's not feeling cold yet, but he's not wearing his combat uniform, just a regular Hydro suit for everyday chores and light training classes, so he knows it has limitations. It's not built to protect his body from exposure to such a climate as this. Not to mention that the bottom part of his pants is soaked through.

He's wearing ankle boots underneath, but now the cold is seeping up higher, creeping up towards his knees, and he's feeling it penetrate his clothes.

Still he keeps running, his legs pumping the soft snow in a steady beat, his knees a perfect ninety degrees to his straight back, his mind distracted by the colors of the sky. He lifts his eyes to catch a glimpse of it again, although he hates himself for his weakness, and it's gone.

He didn't remember that.

The sunset doesn't last above half an hour, of course, he knew that. Now the sky seems to descend upon the trees, its color dark blue, a few stars and satellites beginning to stud the horizon.

"Oomph."

For the second time in a day, Felix feels his chest contract with something solid and falls flat on his face.

The bear has stopped short and it's growling in an angry, plaintive voice that sounds almost human. Felix has had enough. He gets up, more slowly this time, and swipes the goggles around his neck, flinging them on the ground.

Immediately the world around him turns a bit darker, but everything comes into sharp focus. He wipes his brow with the back of his hand, discovering that his hair is damp with sweat.

He opens his mouth to swear again, and that's when he sees it. The reason the bear has stopped is that the ground gives way at this point. Right beneath Felix's sodden boots the snow turns to ice. There's a lake or whatever this kind of large body of water is called, starting right here. It's frozen, like everything else in this timer place. And there's a gaping hole in its middle, about twenty feet from where Felix and the bear are standing.

Infinite blue is surrounding him, the calmness caressing his ears and the cold is stinging his uncovered eyes. Behind him the bear huffs and puffs and gets on his nerves.

Then, a splash shatters the silence. A small hand grabs the jagged edge of the broken ice, and promptly slides back in the water with a quiet flop.

Felix feels his eyes try to jump out of his face.

Then he's running, slipping on the ice, falling on his chest as he's been taught and crawling on all fours towards the lake. The small hand appears again, struggling to latch on to the ice before it's submerged again, but Felix was close this time and he saw.

He saw it's covered in blood.

six

tin soldier

Felix clambers to the hole, crawling on his stomach across the ice, pushing himself forward with all he's got. He's panting a little, but his heart is beating normally -which is hardly at all- so he's fine. He's been trained to do these little mental checks on his body's condition while he's in a fight, or in extreme survival mode, although he's forgotten to do them until now.

Then the hand appears once more, waving about in the black water, and he flings himself towards it, grabbing it.

The ice beneath his chest gives a loud crack, and he stays absolutely still until it stops. It doesn't break, and Felix leans forward, plunging his arm up to the elbow in the water, holding fast to the hand.

He pulls with all his strength, which is considerable, but the ice is thick and he has to lean down very low, until all the blood rushes to his face and he sees black spots dancing in front of his eyes. His hair flops downward, further obscuring his vision, and it's damp with sweat, clinging to his brow. He curses himself for not having taken one of the last Discs he has in his suit, but all that takes place in the back of his mind.

The front is busy pulling a girl out of the freezing water.

The dark curls at the top of her head, heavy with water, drip on his sleeve, as her chin just barely breaks the surface. She coughs out a wet, gurgling scream and lifts her white face to his. He only has time to see how huge her eyes are and how blue her lips have turned before she loses her grip on his glove, which has been made sleek with water, and slips soundlessly under once more. A curse escapes his lips.

"No!" he yells.

Without thinking twice about it, he brings his hand to his mouth and grips the glove between his front teeth, tearing it from its strap around his wrist. Then he spits it away from him, not caring where it lands, and leans down once more, his other hand braced on the ground.

The little girl flounders to the surface once more, her mouth opening in a silent gasp, filling with water, and he manages to grab her hair.

"Grab my hand, take it!" he shouts, but the girl doesn't hear him, or if she does, she can't move.

Gasping, Felix takes off his other glove in the same way, and sticks both hands in the water, leaning so far down that one false move will land him in the water, right beside her. He finds purchase with his boots on the ice, and leans in, moving his arm carefully in the water, until it meets something solid. He pulls again, this time with a firmer grasp on her sleeve, and feels her weight shift.

He swears and tugs harder.

"Come on, hold on to me," he says, but nobody is listening.

It takes forever to lift her face clear out of the water, and when he does he notices that she isn't fighting any longer. Her weight feels dead in his arms, and he drags her upwards once more, absently noticing that his arms are beginning to shake with panic.

The cold is stinging at his fingers, and he practically can't feel his hands now that he's taken the gloves off; he doesn't even know where he threw them. A few days ago, these things would have been all he could think about.

Right now, all he cares more about is how to get a good grip under the girl's armpits, so that she won't slide back in as he lifts her to him. He leans her down on the ice, her legs still dangling in the water. The ice below him doesn't seem to have a mind to start breaking again, so, without taking the time to carry her all the way onto solid land, he leans down to place his palms flat on her chest and starts pumping.

He's almost sure that she's dead, but then, just as he's bending over her face to push her lips apart with his fingers, as he was taught in Health Tech, she jerks upwards and spits out a small trickle of water, hacking and struggling to breathe. She turns those huge eyes towards him and notices his hand still on her chest, his fingers reaching towards her lips.

Then two things happen simultaneously.

One is that she lifts her bleeding arm and slaps him roundly on the left cheek.

The other is that he realizes she's not a child: she's a young woman.

A woman, as in, someone who isn't allowed to be touched by a man, much less a soldier, on penalty of high treason. A woman, like one of the creatures he's only seen in Projections -apart from 'Mother', but she wasn't a real woman, as he found out later- and who live in Segments in the Lower Quarters and the Working Settlements in the Islands, doing menial labors and donating... whatever it is they donate so that people can be created.

"You..." he says intelligently, feeling the bitter taste of the river water on his lips as it's dripping from his hair.

"Stupid Drone," the girl murmurs, turning her face away from him. "You're all the same." Then she coughs some more until he's almost sure she'll drown right in front of his eyes, on dry land, and tries to pull her legs up from the hole.

Drone.

He's only heard that word once before, and it wasn't directed at him. One of the older soldiers, a bearded dude from Europea, once threatened to kill an entire Settlement during a training session. He had missed one of his pills or something. The boys just stood there, the 'Mothers' silent, watching as the kids started cursing at him and throwing bricks that landed dully at their feet.

"Drone!" a little boy, about Karim's age when he first met him, screamed.

His 'Mother' strutted forward to get him inside.

"Freeze!" the bearded soldier had called and she did. "What did you say?" he turned to the boy.

"Drone," the kid repeated. "You're all drones, you've got no brain in your heads. You just take orders from him. The Chairman eat my heart if it isn't true."

Everyone knew that the bearded guy had no choice.

The soldiers have to shoot anyone who speaks treason to the Chairman on sight. That was the price of peace, they all understood it. But when they went back, Felix had been sick right inside the Pod, and had had to spend one week in Infirmary. By the time they let him out, his eyes were hurting.

He didn't want to even blink once -although that was impossible. But every time there was even a hint of darkness around him, he could see the little boy's dead eyes staring him in the face. Only it wasn't just a poor kid in the Hellenic Shores he kept seeing before him. It was Karim. And the soldier with the beard who shot him without a moment's hesitation was he himself.

"Are you in a gang, Drone?" her voice interrupts his thoughts.

The girl -the woman- grunts and tries to move away from him, only it's pathetic, because she can't move an inch, she's so frozen. He gets up on shaky legs, and furrows deeper into his jacket, trying to dispel the sudden coldness that envelopes him, piercing his very bones. Let her freeze, for all he cares.

He's already outside of the law, all he needs is a crazy woman he actually *touched* to add to the pile.

Behind him he can hear her panting, struggling to pull herself up, spitting out water and going nowhere. She's wearing a dress that's torn and clinging to her limbs -it's obviously not made of Hydro. It looks more like the rags they give them in the Desert Pods to wipe their brows with if they get to the point of sweating. He's never had to use one of these, he thinks with pride, until he realizes that he's very much in need of something to wipe his dripping hands and hair right now.

The girl seems to have slipped into unconsciousness beside his feet. A ray of the dipping sun slants so that it hits her hair directly. It glistens in the sudden light in a peculiar, false color. Felix was convinced she was a Colonist, but now he's beginning to think she might have come from the Box. A small pool of blood is beginning to soak the snow under her right arm, where a wound is gaping open.

Her chip. She, or someone else, has taken it out -great. She's a Felon.

"Oh, merc take it," he grumbles as he grabs her other arm and starts pulling her behind him. Her body slides easily on the ice, and he walks like that, not glancing once behind him at her, until they reach the bear.

"Be useful for once, stupid beast," Felix tells it and, as though it understands, it kneels down on all fours so that he can load the girl on its back.

It's only after they've made it to the shack, just as darkness begins to cover the treetops in the distance, making them invisible, that Felix realizes he's left his goggles out on the lake, along with his gloves.

seven

match girl

The girl wakes up in the coldest room she's ever been yet -and she's been in plenty of cold, unforgiving places in her life.

Her teeth are chattering, which she knows is a good sign, but they won't be for long, because she can't feel her legs. Her right arm, although hardly bleeding by this point, is beginning to feel heavy and foreign.

She's still wearing her soaked dress, which chills her skin, the cold piercing her very heart, icy fingers stabbing at her body like daggers.

She's opening her eyes carefully to take in her surroundings, when she remembers the Drone. She sits up abruptly, and almost passes out again from the pain the sudden movement brings on. She fights to stay conscious, wondering when he'll kill her, when she notices something strange.

The Drone is lying on his side on the floor, his face white with pain, his forehead glistening with cold sweat. He's huddled in on himself, his arms wrapped around his knees. He's shaking worse than her, panting in huge shaky breaths, and his eyelids are shut.

"Hey, Drone!" she says, but he doesn't reply. "Wake up."

Nothing.

She drags herself on elbows and knees towards him, her body screaming in pain, and her arm begins to bleed again. She knows she's leaving stains on the lovely carpet as she goes, but she hasn't got anything to wrap it in since she fell through the ice and lost her small stack of provisions along with the quick bandage she had sewn in the water.

She nearly lost her life as well.

'Father... Father Christmas?'

'Constantine...'

She shuts her eyes briefly at the memory of the old man who unknowingly saved her life. And now the Drone did the same, traveling all the way from this huge, icy apartment to the lake, and dragging her from the water.

Although he mustn't have known she was a woman -he'd sooner let her drown than touch her, if he did.

Probably he saw her hair, all natural colored, no synthetics in them, and thought she was a little kid.

"Open your eyes, come on." She's reached the Drone and shakes him violently.

He opens his eyes with difficulty and sees her.

She must look a fright, her hair still dripping, her dress muddy and torn. He looks confused for a second and then he clambers to get away from her, his blue eyes turning huge and scared. She'd laugh if she had the energy.

Merc, he's beautiful.

He must be high-class created, none of the filthy Guards in the Box whom she'd wake up to find bending over her, their dirty fingers always looking for something to grope. His features look like one of the sketches she used to do to amuse the other girls -illegally, of course, and they always asked her where she'd seen men like that.

Well, she hasn't, ever, not quite like that, but she *has* seen actual men, which is more than she can say for the rest of the women.

Even so, she's never seen a boy who looks like that: his face all perfection and no flaws, sharp angles, chiseled cheekbones. Slanting blue eyes, straight nose, full lips. His hair, dyed black at the front, is dripping wet and plastered to his clammy forehead, wheat-blond, thick at the top. Too bad the inside of his head is as empty as the outside is breathtaking.

His body looks slender and hard, his legs incredibly long, his fingers tapered. He's still clad in his Hydro suit, which has molded itself to the planes of his body, outlining every muscle's bulge, as it stretches with his every shallow breath. He's just lying there, immobile, his arms on the floor, stretched out like a fallen eagle's wings.

"Are you stupid?" she mutters. "Do you want to die?"

The Drone doesn't react, so, taking a sharp breath, she lifts herself on her knees and starts taking his jacket off. He feels like a rag doll beneath her fingers, his limbs heavy and helpless and the world goes black around her with the effort. She recovers almost at once -she's been used to being beaten senseless at least once a day, this is nothing- and pulls his other arm out of the jacket.

She lays it aside, and starts doing the same with his pants.

The exercise has warmed her up by the end, which is a good thing, but her toes and fingers are still frozen, and she's also losing more blood, which is not a good thing at all. She won't be able to help him much longer; he'd better start helping himself.

He's now dressed in just a flimsy cotton shirt that stretches across his hard chest and a pair of military blue pants with a red stripe. His feet still in the steel toe boots. She doesn't have the energy to take those off as well. She takes a moment to get her breathing under control, and in a second he's awake.

"What did you...?" He leaps off the floor, away from her, as though she's contaminated him -and who knows, maybe she has.

He's shaking still, but his cheeks are red, heat beginning to creep inside him.

"Your Hydro suit," she says with difficulty, because suddenly it hurts to breathe. "It was killing you. It was trying to reverse your body's reaction, but it ended up freezing you completely. In a second it would have knocked you out cold. It's not made for temperatures as low as these." She tries to take a deep breath, but there doesn't seem to be enough space in her chest for air. "Who do you think makes your suits?" she mutters under her breath.

The Drone drops on all fours and scrambles for his pants.

She tries to give out a shaky laugh, because he looks so funny, all limbs and muscles, his face scared like a little boy's. The laugh ends up choking her, and more water streams out of her nose, but it was totally worth it.

The Drone finds what he was looking for and stands back up.

She hears the familiar click of a gun, and fights down the urge to laugh some more.

"That won't be any use to you, timer Drone," she says, looking up at him from where she's on her knees, on the floor. "I'm dying."

The Drone looks surprised.

Do they have feelings still? she wonders. She feels everything going dark again, but makes one last effort to speak.

"Does this palace have a match?" she asks.

"What?" he says stupidly.

"Matches," she repeats. "We need to light a fire, or we're both for Mercury."

It's a myth that when you die you go to Mercury, the most obscure and unexplored corner of the Solar System. It's a lie of course, like all myths. She's seen what happens to people with they die.

Pain and betrayal and then nothingness.

That's death and she's almost welcoming it.

"Do you know what twenty-five twenty-five is?" she asks suddenly, remembering the old man's last words. He didn't seem afraid to die. Just infinitely sad. "I don't know anything about the sciences, but it sounds like letters. Or... numbers, I think."

Her head falls back, cracking on the hard floor, and then she must die at last, for the next thing she knows is nothingness.

She wakes up in another room, something pressing on her so violently that the breath leaves her lungs with a 'whoosh'.

She opens her eyes -merc, even her eyelids hurt excruciatingly- to find the Drone's eyes inches from her face, his hands on her chest.

"Again?" she murmurs.

Then she feels her head being lifted by his

hand behind her neck, and she'd love to hit him some more, only she can't move her arms. Definitely not good.

His eyes are a dark blue, boring into hers, frantic. "Good, you're awake."

She takes a breath, which catches in her throat. "Not good for you," she tries to say, but it ends up sounding like a gurgle. The Drone shakes her again, and she coughs out water. He leans above her and she thinks, that's it, he's going to whip out his gun again.

"Help me," he whispers through white lips.

He's still shaking, she can see.

Still, he must be feeling a bit better, because he's dragged her all the way to another room. He's holding out a black tin box, right in front of her.

"Timer stuff," she whispers, letting her head flop back. "Open it."

He looks a bit confused, probably because the box has no button, but he works it out in the end.

This room is quaint, filled with Old Time objects. Everything is in perfect condition as far as she can tell. How have all these things been preserved so well for such a long time? Most of the stuff in here is from before the Revision, which was what? About the time she was born. The obsolete table is clean. There's actual real windows and things hung on the walls and... is that a...?

She struggles to lift herself up to look better, and immediately his hand supports her back. She leans against his strength without thinking of it. His hands are freezing.

"That's it," she says when she sees it.

There's a furnace-heater in the corner.

The Drone leans her back down, and places the tin box in her fingers. Then he gets up.

The thing must easily be two decades old, maybe more. It's a timer heater, complete with a little grate underneath and a plastic hoop that radiates heat when it works. The Drone reaches it and lifts it easily in one hand -it must be light, it's made mostly out of plastic, after all, still it can't be that weightless. It isn't very tall; it comes up to his knees. Also, it isn't charged. The light next to the button is dark. He brings it next to her, right where she's lying on the floor.

"It can't have working autonomous batteries," he gasps, "it looks like timer junk. What are these lumps?"

The coals, he means. They're synthetic, not real, still they need to be ignited somehow... The tin box is open and she struggles to see inside past her blurring vision. There's a few little timer cups -porcelain they called it- and an old plastic container of brown cookies. Then, yes! Matches.

She takes them out with shaking fingers, and tries them one by one.

She pushes her finger against the brown edge

and on the other end there's a red edge that's supposed to light up. But only if there's any of the timer gas left in them. The first five little cylinders are out of gas. She picks the sixth one - there's ten in here- but her fingers won't obey her.

"Hey hey, stay with me." The Drone is next to her. "I'll do it, just tell me what to do."

"Press it with your finger until it's warm," she says. "Then it has to light up."

"It doesn't." He sounds desperate, close to tears.

She lifts a hand to indicate the next one.

He tries the last three.

"None of them do anything," he says quietly.

She lies back again. "I'm sorry," she says in the same tone. The cold is getting better now. Just as it did when she was in the water, one of the last times she tried to raise her hand out and grab the ice. She knows what this means. Maybe the Drone isn't so stupid after all, because he seems to understand too.

He lays down beside her, his body parallel to hers, although his boots reach out almost to the other wall, that's how tall he is. He gasps, trying to breathe through the numbness.

"I'm Felix," he says, his breath a white cloud.

"Are you serious?" she replies, her eyes suddenly alert.

'Constantine. Twenty-five twenty-five. Felix,

my hope.'

"As the plague," he says, his voice growing faint. "Oh, and in case you end up dying with the question unanswered... Twenty-five twenty-five would be the new year that's coming in ten days. We are now in year twenty-five twenty-four. Not that you'd know that five goes after four. Hey, what's that?"

He must be losing his mind, she thinks. Cold can do that to you. Death can as well.

"What?" she asks. She's so tired, she could sleep forever.

"Found it in the box, next to the 'matches'. Useless thing, looks like the rest, but it has no room for gas. No button, either. Looks like a tiny piece of wood."

He brings it in front of her eyes. Freezing limbs and all, she lifts her head up so quickly all the blood rushes from her face. She takes a small breath, steadying herself.

"Give me your boot."

"My..."

"Bring your leg over, do it," she says quickly.

Looking at her like she's crazy, the Drone - Felix- bends his knee with difficulty. She grabs the match -this is a simple match, like they used in ancient times, no gas, no nothing, just rub it on a rough surface and it catches on fire. Not everything has been made better with time. She drags it across the rough leather of his military boot. With a hissing sound, it sparkles to life. The smell of burnt wood fills her nostrils.

She gets on her knees, reaching the heater, and he places a hand on her elbow, steadying her. She pushes the button that opens the drawer underneath, where the grate is, and drops the flaming match right on the chemical coals. Immediately they catch on fire, and Felix flings the door shut, although she doubts he's ever seen real fire in his life.

She has, though.

The bottom part of the heater starts sprouting flames. Sparks fly to the carpet, land on her dress, but she doesn't care. Instead of taking a step back, she huddles closer, making room for the soldier. Warmth starts to seep into her skin, the heater's hoop turning red with it, and that's when the pain starts.

She didn't think she'd mind so much, but maybe her body is sick and tired of all the torment she's been inflicting it to lately, because a small whimper escapes her lips before she can stop it.

Next thing she knows, the soldier has grabbed her by the throat, and is forcing his fingers into her mouth. She struggles to break free, biting and turning her head this way and that, but he's so much stronger than her that he doesn't budge an inch. He finally takes his fingers out of her mouth, and presses it shut with one hand below her nose and the other under her chin.

She struggles to breathe, but she can't, and panicking, she swallows. There's a bitter taste in her mouth where he forced his fingers, and it makes her gag to think of what he's trying to do to her, but suddenly she feels her whole body going slack.

"Good girl," the Drone murmurs somewhere in the distance. "Brainless, but obedient."

"I'm not the one that was nearly killed by my own clothes," she wants to say, but her lips have gone numb. "What did you do to me?"

She can't say that either.

She fought her way out of the Box, out of grief, and out of the frozen water, only to die beside the first sparkling fire she's made in days. That's what this world is all about, isn't it, though?

No matter how hard you fight, that's what it all amounts to. Nothing.

At least she'll see her father again.

She's been missing him so much it hurts to breathe.

eight

tin soldier

The Felon girl slips into unconsciousness right before his eyes. There was such a look of sadness on her face right after he made her swallow his last green striped Disc that his heart almost broke.

But just before her eyes drifted shut there was a smile on her face.

She's out of it now.

Felix lays down beside her again, feeling the warmth coming from the timer device spread to his legs, his arms, his chest. His skin is on fire. So that's what flames look like in real life.

He can't imagine how his goggles could ever make this red and orange and blue color look any more vibrant. The flames are dancing this way and that, threatening to escape the metal cage of the heater, but never quite reaching as far as the girl's fingers, which are still curled against the drawer where she threw the lit match.

The tip of her second finger is black with soot.

Her hair is beginning to dry out, spread out in

a cloud around her head, the exact color of the flames. He's never seen hair like that. It's touching him, too. Strands of it are strewn across his shoulder, and one curl has tangled itself on his palm, which is still grabbing the back of her neck.

The pill will heal her injury, he's almost certain. It will close up her skin. Plus, she was who knows how long in the water, and obviously she's swallowed a lot. She might even have contacted the plague out there.

Hopefully his body is strong enough to heal without the pill. Hopefully.

The bear scratches the door outside, making its presence known.

What a day he's had.

Not even the most gruesome training fortnight on the Himalayas can be compared to this. And why is his brain so fuzzy all of a sudden? Did the Felon manage to give him a disease already?

Merc, he should have left her there. He shouldn't have even gotten out of the shack. Karim must be thinking he's dead by now. He's taken the tracker off his ear, and it can't work unless it's in contact with human skin, but sooner or later someone will think of his fascination with the North Pole, and they'll find their way up here.

And what about the Clock?

What in the timers will he do with the Clock? If it's as important as the Vis implied, then he's in for much more trouble than touching a girl and harboring a Felon. A Felon with hair like flames.

His thoughts become jumbled together, and, without realizing it, right there in the Old Time kitchen of the Clockmaster's ice shack, next to a girl that doesn't know how to count and is probably wanted for high treason, Felix falls asleep for the first time in his life.

He doesn't have time to freak out about what's happening to him.

He doesn't have the strength to question it.

He just slips into a deep, healing sleep, the first of his life, with the fire cracking merrily in the Old Time heater next to him, as the world outside the window settles for another icy Arctic night.

nine

tin soldier

He wakes up hungry as a wolf.

There are gunshots ringing through the walls, and he leaps off the floor, instinctively reaching for the Protector .44 in his suit before he's even properly awake. He's not wearing his suit of course, so his fingers only meet the cotton wool of his pants, and then his body starts screaming at him to lay back down again.

Everything hurts, from his muscles to his joints. And along with the pain the memories start coming back, rushing through his brain, throbbing on his temples. Then again, his head feels oddly quiet, the usual buzz that keeps him on his toes every hour of every day faded to a calmness he's not used to. He doesn't feel groggy, though. Just... present. Alive. That's creepy. What the stars happened to him?

"You fell asleep," an irritating voice calls from the other room.

He bursts through the door, feeling exposed without his Hydro suit, and looks warily around

for his gun. Could she have taken it?
on the floor, her back to him,
Projection on the PR. She's frozen
won't turn around as she continues to speak in
that girlish, annoying tone.

"I don't think you've ever done that before,
have you? We both slept, me because of that foul
thing you forced down my throat. You slept for
more than eleven hours. How do you feel?"

"I..."

How to answer her? If only he had his gun in
his hand, he'd make her realize exactly how he
feels.

"I don't sleep," he ends up saying stupidly.

"You do now," she retorts and passes a small
hand in front of the screen, which explodes with
noise.

That's where the gunshots were coming from.
Felix rubs his temples, feeling faint with hunger.
The girl is dressed all in black.

"Hold on a mercury sec," bursts from his lips
as he strides forward, reaching her in two steps.
He was right. Dammit.

She's put on the Clockmaster's black cloak, his
good one, the one he wears only once a year, for
the Perennial Celebration. He's seen in countless
times on the Channel. Three days ago, when he
transmitted here, it was the first thing he looked
for. He remembers the shiver that ran down his
spine as he touched it, wishing he could see the

Clockmaster with his own eyes, just once, running his hands across the shiny, silky texture like through water. And then he searched every inch of it for a hidden pocket, a compartment, anything that might contain the 'further instructions' the old madman had promised him.

He found nothing.

Now the girl just sits there, her small frame dwarfed by the black material, her hair sticking up in all directions, so red it hurts his eyes.

"What in the timers do you think-?" he stops abruptly.

Another gunshot rings in the PR, and the girl's shoulders droop, shaking. Felix's breath dies in his throat.

It's an old Vis she's watching, one from the Terrestrial Channel. It's not even news, it happened two years ago, he thinks.

That man, the pirate, what was his name? Christopher Steadfast. It was plastered all over the news for months. He hijacked a fleet of the One World intergalactic shuttles, stock-full of air-warfare, murdered the commander pilot, and changed the coordinates so that they all crashed somewhere in the Pacific Ocean. It was supposed to be a suicide mission, and he was supposed to have drowned along with the First Plane, the only one who had a commander -the rest were manned by stimulations, not humans. But they were waiting for him as soon as the ship's hull hit the water.

President Kun was beside himself for days, because this was a multi-billion loss for the One World, but he couldn't do a damn thing about it while the fleet was hurtling through space to the earth's atmosphere. What he could do was send a team of men to dig through the carcass of the First Plane and bring up Steadfast, more dead than alive. They revived him, and brought him back to the excellent health every citizen of the One Word enjoys.

And then what is known as the Fortnight of Terror began.

It was called so originally because Steadfast was said to be the head of a terrorist gang, but as soon as it became obvious that the pirate wasn't going to talk no matter what they did to him, his ordeal went viral. Every day the Terrestrial Channel would broadcast a couple new Projections about what was being done to him.

They cast him off on a deserted island, near the oil rigs in the Caribbean, without any pills or one stitch of Hydro to protect his skin from the scorching sun. The whole One World watched as he became emaciated and sick with fever; still he did not surrender. Then they took him to the Box.

Felix hates to admit it, but he didn't watch most of the Visuals from then on. They did inhuman things to him. Of course what Steadfast had done had been inhuman too, more than inhuman, it had jeopardized the One World's peace directly, making the Planet vulnerable so that the Colonies would be able to contest Chairman Kun's position. That would lead to wars of such proportions that the Revision would seem like child's play.

Everyone knew that.

Everyone knew that Steadfast and his colleagues deserved everything that had happened to him two years ago.

Even so, it was unbearable to watch as they filled his veins with electricity or gave him shots of canine DNA, the effects of which lasted for at least five hours at a time. It was pure torture just watching him. Steadfast didn't breathe a word about who or what or where his friends were.

By the end of the Fortnight of Terror he was mad. He kept pointing to the sky and yelling meaningless syllables and among them one word. It sounded like a code name. 'Astra.' They searched high and low for that thing, or person, or whatever it was -Felix himself was head of several such expeditions. 'Operations A' they were called, and they were relentless. Anyone who refused to give them information was immediately charged with high treason. That's how important 'Astra' was. After months and months of combing the Planet, they ended up with nothing but lose ends and no conclusive evidence as to where to go next.

On the floor, the girl is watching, soundless. The Projection has reached the point where the soldiers catch up to Steadfast in the Caribbean island as he's running on the sand, his skin badly sunburned, his body skeletal. He drops to his knees, his head hanging between his shoulders as though he's tired of keeping it upright, and a young soldier -practically a kid- approaches him and presses a magnetic rod to his neck, which floods his body with almost 1,000 volts. The pirate's eyes roll back in his head and his body convulses, kicking up sand and seawater. The soldiers take a step back as though he's dangerous. Felix turns his eyes away. He doesn't know what disturbs him more.

Watching Steadfast being fried alive, and knowing he woke up after that only to be fried again and again and again? The fact that in the Projection, he suddenly notices how young Steadfast looks? So young and handsome, what's left of his muscles bulging like his own, his hair a mop of vibrant color, his eyes dark and mysterious -he can't be older than thirty five, if that.

Or that the soldier who pushes the magnetic rod into his throat is dark-skinned, shiny-eyed, and bulky?

It's Karim.

The girl is shaking really badly by now, as though the electricity entered her own body.

She lifts a hand to swipe in front of the PR, but it's shaking so much the screen can't obey her. Felix leans forward and freezes it for her, just as Steadfast wakes up and starts screaming. He cuts him off mid-scream, feeling a chill run down his back.

"Are you-?" he starts to ask the girl, but then she turns around to face him and he stops.

Her face is stark white in contrast to her dark curls, her eyes pools of infinite sadness. Water is streaming down her cheeks -tears. He hasn't seen anyone cry. The mere sight of it freezes him. The girl is staring straight into his eyes, making not one sound, while her swollen lips, wet with tears, are gulping in shuddering breaths.

Why on mars would she watch this thing?

Why?

Then she speaks five words, and he knows why. His eyes stray to her right arm, which was bleeding a few hours ago, now clean, only a slight scar indicating where her personal chip was embedded before she tore it out.

He drops his head in his hands, just standing there in front of the weeping girl, the accusations shooting from her eyes, reaching his chest, opening him up like a crimson wound.

"Were you one of them?" is what she said.

"No," he says in a choked voice. "No, I wasn't."

He could very well have been, though. Karim was one of the team. He was the one who...

"I'll watch it all," she says, interrupting his thoughts. "I don't think you want to stay."

"Why?"

She shrugs. "I haven't seen it in three months," she says. Does the stupid girl put on the Fortnight of Terror every month? he wonders. Is that what she means? "I miss him," she adds, not taking her eyes off his face.

"Oh." Felix says cleverly. He still doesn't get it. And then, out of the blue, he does. "*Oh*," he breathes, horrified. "Are you... are *you* Astra?"

ten

match girl

The first time he says her name, it sounds like a curse on his lips. It's been a curse on everyone's lips in the two years since her father's murder.

"Of course I am," she tells him quietly, wiping her cheeks. "What did you idiot Drones think an 'Astra' was? His criminal accessory? His next terrorist device? His secret army of intelligent droids? He was calling for his merking daughter as he was *dying*!"

She spits the last word out and he flinches.

"They knew what he meant, you know, just as soon as he said it," she goes on. "They didn't wait for him to say it twice, before they had me in the Box. Then they fed you all these lies, and had you searching for... what was it? Weeks? Months? Years?"

"Six months," the soldier tries to say, but his lips have gone dry.

"Well, they kept me in the Box for two years, and finally they brought me up here to kill me. I turned sixteen three days ago. They let me loose and expected me to drop dead from cold and hunger, and when I didn't they hunted me down like an animal. They finally shot me and killed me, only it wasn't me."

"Huh?"

"It was an old man, he..." her throat catches. "I don't think they expected anyone to be walking out in the snow, except for the girl they'd left in the cold to die. Only I didn't die from the cold. I've learnt to survive without pills. Eat, light a fire, put myself to sleep... that sort of thing."

"Did he have blue eyes like mine?" the soldier asks with urgency and Astra looks at him with surprise.

Does he know the old man? Is this...? Oh no. This can't be *his* house!

She looks straight into the soldier's eyes.

They're the exact color of the sky at the moment when twilight has just began to fall, and the first star is shining on the horizon. Suddenly she shudders, feeling as though she's looking into the old man's eyes.

They're identical.

The memory floods her as though it happened a moment ago. She feels again the rough texture of the old man's hand as she held it in hers, freezing with cold; she sees the pool of blood draining from his chest, where he was shot. She sees his eyes focus for a minute on Ursa the bear, and she feels her heart dripping with sadness that he didn't even have the time to look at the last, magnificent polar bear clearly, the beast that came to her rescue when she was dying of cold, and that she named Ursa after her favorite constellation.

How such an animal has survived all this time is beyond her. The very species has been pretty much extinct for decades, only a few specimens are left, which are in the care of the Intergalactic Research Facilities, studied for their genetic material and abilities.

When the ice cracked beneath her feet, about three days after she watched the old man being buried beneath the thickly falling snow, she thought that was it. She had gulped down icy water along with her panic, and had tried to hold on to the jagged ice for as long as she could, screaming in pain from the cold that pierced her every bone. She slipped under more times than she cares to remember.

The mere memory of the numbing water closing over her head is enough to make her shudder. The minutes she survived in that hole were the worst she's spent yet. Even counting the times in the Box she would open her eyes to a Drone bending over her, pushing his way between her legs -or watching her father die on the Terrestrial Channel over and over, just so that she could see him one last time.

How had the bear known to run fetch the

soldier?

Astra swallows hard.

The blue eyes that are watching her are stormy, and she knows the soldier is reaching his breaking point. She can't imagine what must be going through his head; there's a whole world opening up before him, a world that has been carefully kept hidden from him his entire life.

As she was watching her father on the PR, she could feel him rigid with shock behind her, even though she didn't turn to look at him. I should watch it again, she thinks. He should watch it with me. He should wake up.

It's time.

He looks smart enough now that he's missed a pill or two, who knows how he'll become after he runs around in the cold a little? Maybe there's some sort of actual human behind this handsomely crafted façade.

'Did he have blue eyes like mine?'

"Not quite as vacant and stupid as yours," she replies, "but yes, he did. I held his hand as he was dying."

eleven

tin soldier

"What have you done?" Felix grabs her by the shoulders and shakes her. When did everything stop making sense? He feels lightheaded; he sways on his feet. "That was the Clockmaster, that was my... that was the Clockmaster," he finishes lamely.

The girl -the wanted girl, Astra- gets to her feet and shuts the PR down.

"You need to eat," she says curtly.

His hand goes absently to his button for the last two pills, and then he remembers he doesn't have his jacket on. He finds it draped on the sofa, but Astra has beaten him to it. She's rather fast on her feet, although now that she's standing up he can see that she's built very small, like a child. How can such a small person cause so much chaos?

She grabs the pills and walks into the other room.

"Hey, where are you going? Stop!" he rushes after her only to catch a glimpse of the back of her hand as she's feeding them to the fire. "No no no no-" he runs after her, panicked. "Don't..." but it's too late, of course. His last resources for sustenance are gone. That's that.

His head is pounding.

"That's not food, that's poison," Astra says, sweeping past him, the Clockmaster's cloak pooling at her feet. "Put on your jacket or whatever it is you tin soldier wimps call those things, and follow me. We wouldn't want you to freeze to death again."

He reaches out an arm to block her exit.

"What," he asks dangerously, his voice threateningly calm, "did you call me?"

"Oh," she says, "haven't you been called that before? 'A tin soldier'. It's what all of us girls used to call you in the dorms after hours. Because... you know, your heart doesn't beat. I didn't know it back then, but it turns out that those pills you 'eat' to fix your injuries or instead of food or whatever, well, they slow down your heart and your brain so that..."

"So that *what*?" someone asks furiously.

It turns out it's him.

Astra lets out a little laugh. "So that you don't have overpowering emotions or needs or the other things that make a human being human. My father was a chemist, before they dubbed him a 'terrorist' and 'the pirate', one of the best on the Planet. Did you know that?"

Tears have started rolling down her cheeks again. He feels his fingers curling into fists.

"He used to work for Chairman Kun, in some kind of highly classified capacity. Top secret projects. Your pills were one of them, that's how he found out the truth. You have no heart, Drone boy. You're a tin soldier."

"Big words from a match girl," he retorts.

He knows it's childish, calling her names, but he can't make himself stop. The girl just laughs. It's a strange sound, bouncing off the walls of the house, ringing in his ears long after she's stopped. He doesn't like how it unsettles him, right there, in the pit of his stomach, which, stomach, by the way, gives out a low rumble.

"Right," Astra says. "Food." She turns and heads for the door.

"Oh no," Felix says, "I'm not going back out there," at the same time that the green door is flung open and a blast of icy air hits him in the face.

"Ursa!" Astra yells at the top of her lungs.

"Hey! Just pierce my eardrum while you're at it."

Felix wonders why he hasn't shot the girl by now. Then he glances outside and his breath catches.

The morning is glorious, white and blue and yellow, sunlight streaming through a thick layer of grey clouds, a light frosting of snowflakes drifting from the sky.

"Are you coming or not?" Astra's irritating little voice sounds as though it's coming from the sky itself. Then he turns and sees her perched on top of the merking bear.

"Where did that come from?" he starts to ask, but stops short when he notices a small hand reaching down to him. Her eyes are holding a challenge as though she doubts that he'll have the guts to follow.

He climbs nimbly up on the beast's back, without touching her hand. The animal's fur sways with the wind beneath his legs, and he gets a little dizzy with the bear's every movement. It's not rhythmic like the machines he's used to. It's entirely unpredictable.

"Hold on to me," Astra says, as though he would even consider touching her. "And where is your jacket? You'll freeze."

"So will you," he retorts stubbornly. He'll be damned before he's called a 'tin soldier wimp' for wearing his Hydro jacket again. "And, by the way, you forgot to thank me for saving your life."

The bear raises itself on all fours and begins to walk slowly towards the trees. Felix feels a shiver of anticipation. He doesn't even notice the cold. All he can see is little individual snowflakes landing against the Clockmaster's black cloak and melting on Astra's red hair. He can't take his eyes off it.

He can feel her heart pounding through her back, against his chest. She's panting, but not in pain as she was yesterday. She's excited. She's vibrating with life, making him feel as though he's been living everything from behind his goggles.

Well, he has, but metaphorically.

His own heart hasn't beat more than twenty times in a minute since he came out of the Box - not that he can feel its beats. They're normally very slow and quiet. This wasn't always so in the history of humanity, but now, thanks to the Revision and the Health Discs, hearts can last longer. They beat less, so they don't exhaust themselves like the timers' hearts used to do. It has been one of the greatest achievements of the Chairman and his Revision.

Tin soldier. Ugh. The stupid match girl is beginning to get under his skin.

How stupid to ask for thanks for saving her life. She won't even acknowledge she heard him.

"Oh, no need to thank you," Astra says lightly right at that moment, flinging the words over her shoulder with a careless gesture. "I'll save yours right back."

t w e l v e

This beast was certainly not built to accommodate passengers, Felix thinks a few hours later, standing once more inside the shack, in front of the PR, rubbing his sore leg muscles and deliberating whether what he's about to do is one of the stupidest things ever.

"Well?" Astra says, coming into the room.

She's wiping her hands on a flimsy piece of material. "Hold on," he replies, annoyed again. "I didn't say I'll play it. I just said I *might*."

"You *might* have started to get on my nerves," she says sweetly. He doesn't retort this time. Not that she'll let him act superior for once. "I know I'm getting on yours," she adds.

A curse flies out of his lips.

He never used to curse so much. In fact, he rarely did at all. The other soldiers said words like that all the time, when they were goaded past their endurance, past their strength and patience -although in most classes it's forbidden.

He doesn't think he's ever been tested past his

endurance. Until now.

"Come on, come on, come oooon," Astra says, sounding exactly like Karim. When he was four.

Felix had his first meal today. Real food, that is.

His stomach still feels weird.

He's got a strange taste in his mouth, and he's not sure he liked tasting the flesh of an actual animal -if it hadn't been a matter of survival he would never have touched that half charcoal, half freezing cold piece she put in front of him. But the match girl insisted that it was 'cooked' whatever *that* meant, and his Sergeant always says that survival comes before anything else.

Survival at all costs. It's a military motto.

Felix pretends to fumble with the controls on the PR, while in his mind he's recreating the Fortnight of Terror -the scene in the Caribbean Astra was watching yesterday.

The pirate didn't put survival above anything else. He remembers Astra's bleeding little hand bursting through the surface of the ice before flopping back in the water. She didn't put survival above all either. But did they have another choice? Does he?

"Am I waiting for something?"

Merc, is this girl impatient or what? "I don't know, are you?" he spits at her. She stomps from the room.

Great.

He flops cross-legged to the ground. He supposes he's going to have to start doing a bit of training on his own, now that it's been three days since he's been to school. Already his muscles feel weaker, somehow less than they were. Of course he hasn't taken his Disc for the day. He hasn't taken *any* pill as of last night.

He could so easily freak out right now.

The rode on Ursa's back -that bear shouldn't even be here, now she has a name? anyway- for hours. It probably was less than one hour, but still it felt like hours. The beast kept swaying and breaking into a run and tossing its head as though it had no thought for its passengers. And of course it didn't. This used to be a wild animal, attacking humans and other animals, which of course don't exist either by now, not merking carrying them on its back.

Still Astra, or rather Astra's back, looked perfectly calm.

It swayed along with the beast easily, as though she was a part of it, a continuation of its body. She didn't look cold either, again from what he could tell from her black-cloaked back, but he had to grit his teeth and force his body to relax. He was almost thrown countless times.

When they arrived -they arrived nowhere, by the way, but Astra seemed certain that 'it was here'- he thought he saw a small smile curling on her lips, but she quickly turned around and hid it as he was tumbling down from the bear's back.

"Now what?" he asked sullenly.

"Now we stalk," she replied, while the bear walked on, but Astra didn't follow.

"You don't even know what stalking is," he scoffed. That was a military term; what was it doing coming out of her mouth?

"No, *you* don't know what stalking is," she retorted. Always with the last word, this girl. "Nobody knew what it was, back in the ancient days. Humans learnt it from animals. This, my friend, is where it all started. It's in their nature."

She was watching the slow-moving beast, mesmerized.

"Did you say 'my friend'?" he murmured, biting his lip so that he wouldn't laugh.

"Shut up," she said.

Then they proceeded to freeze for who knows how long, until Ursa suddenly stuck her front paw into a tiny hole in the ice, which Felix hadn't even noticed before, and flung something small and moving right at Astra's feet. Astra, with a small squeak of joy picked up the slimy, flopping thing in her arms and stuck it in front of his nose.

It smelled foul. Felix fought not to gag.

"That's a fish," she said as though it was an epiphany. "A carp, I believe."

"I know what it is," he replied, although he really didn't. It looked so different in real life.

And it smelled so disgusting. "Polar bears don't eat fish," he added, on a sudden impulse of showing-off his knowledge of Old Time wildlife.

"They do when all other form of life is extinct," she said dryly, as though it was somehow his fault. "It's going to taste like a little bit of cloud, trust me. Here."

She was actually holding the Clockmaster's cloak open for him. It was obvious that he was shivering, of course, as it was obvious that the cloak could fit them both inside, as well as half of Ursa. But he wouldn't even consider sitting so close to the girl, being...

"Come on, no-heart," she said. "Don't be a no-brains as well."

He sat as far from her as he could, but it still wasn't far enough. At least it was warmer inside the cloak, although part of it was her body heat that floated between their almost-touching arms, like a visible thing. They waited some more. A lot more.

Astra got up and started running in place, just a few yards back and forth, back and forth. She looked like a crazy person. In a few minutes he got up and joined her.

Then, when they both had had enough lunacy for one day, and Ursa had flung five more disgusting fish out of the hole, they started for home.

Astra marched into the Clockmaster's ice

shack, which, by the way, she was still calling 'a palace' and stupid things like that, with one of the fish, tossing the rest to the bear.

"You realize you've been giving the evil eye to your food all day, don't you?" she told him.

After burning it on the heater for a few minutes, and stinking up the entire three rooms of the shack, she cut it into two uneven pieces, and put them in plates onto the table. "Sit down, your majesty," she told him and then, without waiting, she started to stuff the thing in her mouth, making satisfied noises.

He still doesn't know how he managed to get it past his lips, let alone keep it down. He can feel it in his stomach, like an actual thing descended down there with every bite. He feels his belly full for the first time in his life. Of course he's still ravenously hungry, but at least he doesn't feel as though he's going to pass out every time he gets up from a chair.

She made him swallow a lot of water, too, voluntarily. He still doesn't know why on Jupiter he listened to her. It tasted cold and clear and wet. It made him feel better, though, sort of fuller, plus his head isn't hurting anymore.

Astra then proceeded to 'wash' the plates, whatever that meant, and he swallowed his pride and disgust and told her: "Thank you for the... fish."

"You need to pay me," she said.

"Eh?" he said.

"With a story," she explained.

Which landed him in this mess.

thirteen

match girl

The soldier finally decides to turn on the Vis his grandfather or the Clockmaster or someone sent him -she's not clear on what exactly is going to happen here. All she knows is he promised he'd show her the reason he's here, in this 'frozen hole at the top of the planet' -his words- and outside of the law.

Astra stifles a scoff, but he hears it, and tells her that 'practically everybody must be looking for him by now.'

She tells him that he's full of himself and he turns his back to her and starts the Vis.

The face of the old man hits her like a punch in the stomach.

She feels tears stinging her eyes and she hates that. She never cries, except when she watches her father being tortured in the playback from the Terrestrial Channel.

"That's him," she feels necessary to say, her voice shaking a little. She hopes he doesn't notice, but of course, he does. "That's the old man who died instead of me."

"I know," he answers after a second. He sounds as though he's about to lose it. "Just watch this."

She finds out that he was nearly two hundred years old. She finds out that he had secrets -who doesn't, these days? And most important of all, she finds out that the look in his blue eyes, his eyes that look so young and alive in his weathered face, those brilliant, intelligent eyes that haven't been dulled by the One World's pills or any of the other new inventions they've built their lies on... The look in his eyes is the same as the one her father has in the Projection, that first time he wakes up after being electrocuted in the Caribbean.

If you take out the excruciating pain, that is.

It's fear.

Fear and love, all knotted together in a single glance.

Actually, that's not exactly what she sees. It's not fear *and* love. It's fear *for* something that he loves.

Strange, that.

She didn't think, after her father died, that there was anybody else alive who had something to love -something to lose. Just at that point the old man, Ulysses, drops another bomb. He's the Drone's grandfather.

Turns out she's not the only one with a father in the whole One World.

"It's ok," Felix says softly.

"Would you stop talking, I'm trying to think," she snaps at him. The Vis has ended, but she's pretending to be thinking it over. There' not much to think over, of course, since she barely understood anything from what the old man said. But that's no excuse for the tin soldier to be talking to her all condescending and superior like that.

"It's just that you're... doing it again," he says.

"Doing what?" Why does her throat hurt when she tries to speak, as though it's been scratched raw?

She feels something warm on her cheek and turns around surprised, only to come face to face with him. His eyes fill her vision, so impossibly blue and dark that the breath catches in her throat. His finger is still on her cheekbone, inching closer and closer to her lower eyelash.

"Crying," he whispers.

She wipes her tears, along with his fingers, angrily away.

"Well, *you* were panting the whole time we were on Ursa's back, but I didn't mention it," she says.

He just gets up and goes to the window.

f o u r t e e n

"I'm not the only one with parents," she says after he's given her a moment to compose herself.

"Oh, you are," he replies. "I've got no idea what the Clockmaster -I mean Ulysses is talking about in that thing."

"Clockwhat?" she asks and he laughs.

"Ok, I'm supposing that in the Islands or wherever you grew up, you haven't even heard of the Perennial Celebration..." He knows he said the wrong thing as soon as the words leave his mouth. It is a matter of course that women are raised and then allocated menial jobs exclusively in the Settlements or the Islands, or somewhere along the Coastline of Europea.

It's better to keep them separate from the men, so that's how they've been since the Revision - even before, if history is to be believed.

But right now, as the words come out of his lips, they sound somehow wrong. Why should a girl like her be cut off from the rest of the world? Sure, she's annoying, but that's not a good enough reason to ban her from the rest of the population, is it? Are there more women like her in the Settlements, brave and smart and irritating, confined to the Islands, never to come in contact with anyone but other workers? And more importantly, what business is it of his?

What on mars made thoughts like that pop into his head?

Astra gets up abruptly, and saunters over to stand right next to him.

"We have heard of them," she says, fixing him with her huge, dark eyes. "But that's it. You know women aren't supposed to watch the Channel, except on special occasions, right?"

No, he didn't know.

And if by 'special occasions' she means Steadfast's torture, then... Ah, crap. This is getting more grotesque by the minute.

He starts to answer her, but she's already turned away. She goes to stand closer to the window, and pushes the button to open the shade. Darkness is falling outside by now, so it's not as though the shack is suddenly flooded by light, but still it's pretty disturbing.

Astra just stands in front of the windowpane and stares out into the darkness. What is she looking at?

"It's supposed to bring in the new year," Felix says, "the Clock. In effect, it's a wild celebration that lasts for about ten or so days, and it all begins with the Clock. You know, the one the Clockmaster builds with his actual two hands, no machines involved, no nano-helpers, nothing. The Clo- Ulysses has been building a different Clock every year for at least the past ten years, maybe more. Only a few hundred thousand guests in the entire Planet ever receive an invitation, but I've watched every Perennial for the past six years, and I can tell you, it doesn't get more spectacular than that. The guy was a genius."

"Your grandfather," Astra supplies.

"Well, we'll see about that," Felix says. "Anyway, one year the Clock was hidden inside a huge tent -it's always kept very much secret until the big reveal anyway- and when the flaps opened, the Clock was a huge contraption that started spewing fire and filled the sky overhead with sparks in every color imaginable. Another year it looked like the actual numbers and the hands on it were living creatures, only to be revealed that they was statues carved out of wood. They were working mechanically in a faultless dance -no nanos, remember? The Clockmaster was an engineer back before the Revision, one of the last engineers schooled in the Old Timers' ways. I don't think anyone can do what he did, I don't think anyone knows how to anymore. He was sort of a link with the Old World, the only timer tradition left, and the Chairman, who always attends the Perennial, gives a grand speech every year about how we are a part of our glorious history and such boring stuff. No one listens to it, but I don't know what would happen if one year the Clockmaster or the Clock weren't there."

"Apparently disaster," Astra murmurs and he can hear it in her voice that she's laughing. "This year, at least."

She's still looking outside, or pretending to, because Felix can't see a thing worth looking at out there.

"What did you say?" he asks with sudden interest.

Astra sighs, as though he's an idiot. "It was his last words, I told you," she says. "And then there's the Vis we just watched. As well as pulling you out of Military school to come here and fix this... Clock. There's only one thing I don't understand, Drone."

"Felix," Felix says. "Wait, there's only *one* thing you don't understand?"

"Have you ever seen the stars so close?" Astra says in a weird, dreamy voice. "They look as though they're about to drop to the earth."

Felix looks out the window, unimpressed. "Those are satellites and the Intergalactic Station Departments," he tells her. "The stars haven't been visible from earth in decades."

"Oh they have been," she says. "If you know where to look. When you see a formation that's irregular, a star that doesn't look ordinary –that's a real star and no satellite."

He sighs. No ordinary star. What does that even mean?

Why are his limbs feeling so heavy? And damn if he isn't hungry again. He feels tired enough that he could just lay down on the floor and close his eyes, let her high-pitched voice fade to oblivion. He's almost sure he's getting sick. What is he doing here, after all? Nothing. If he had a grain of brains left, he would get in the Pod right now and go back to school, merc take the consequences.

"There's nothing *I* understand about Ulysses' Vis," he says, trying to keep the frustration from his voice.

At last she looks away from the fascinating window. "Oh, no, I understood it all. Just one question: what's a Clock?"

Felix looks at her for a stunned second. Then he bursts out laughing.

f i f t e e n

The Drone starts laughing and he can't stop. Astra waits for a second, but the minutes pass and he won't stop howling. She purses her lips. Why can't he control himself a little? He's a tin soldier, for the stars' sake!

Then again, as she watches him right now, gasping for breath, his eyes watering, crinkling at the corners with laughter, he looks more like a human being than he's ever done.

He doesn't look like a Drone at all. He looks... he looks like a Felix. He looks like something only he could be in the entire One World, in the universe. All people used to look like that, once, her father had told her. They used to be like that.

It's one of the few things he taught her. The rest she learned from his comrades.

It takes Felix forever to calm down, and when he does he goes into a jumbled speech of cogwheels and turning hands and minutes and seconds and twenty-four hours in a day.

"I don't think you know what you're talking

about," she tells him and if she can judge from the way his mouth turns into a thin line, he's not too happy about the interruption.

Her stomach is rumbling again. He must be hungry, too.

"I haven't seen a merking Clock in real life, have I?" Felix explodes.

"Have you ever eaten a biscuit?" she asks him. "I mean, they might be older than you, but we'll smell them and if they're good, we can try eating them. I think I saw a packet of them in the box with the matches."

"Of course right now is the time to talk of matches, match girl," he spits out.

"You know, you must learn to control yourself no matter how tired or hungry you are," she tells him sweetly, knowing full well that she's further infuriating him. "Now that chemicals won't take care of your body or your emotions for you, that's just another job you'll have to do."

He looks at her as though she's speaking a foreign language.

"Come on," she tells him walking into the Old Time kitchen room. "We need to clear our heads."

She grabs the biscuits, turning the heater off, since she doesn't want to waste the coals -their energy won't last forever, contrary to what Felix seems to believe. He still hasn't put his Hydro self-heating suit on, and she sort of regrets making that comment about 'tin soldier wimps' but on the other hand she admires his obstinacy.

Well, if he doesn't take it too far.

She opens the green door and the chilling wind slaps her cheeks immediately. It's snowing heavily. She wraps the cloak twice around her body, peering ahead to try to see through the thick curtain of snowflakes.

"Ursa!" she calls, not that she expects the bear to come, but in a second a huge dark mass materializes in the swirling snow, a few steps ahead. She claps her hands in delight.

The bear sits down, sort of lying on her side, and Astra slowly approaches it, furrowing between its legs, relishing in the warmth of its white fur. It smells alive and cold in here; it smells like home.

She opens the plastic packet and brings her nose close to the hard brown biscuits. It smells like nothing. She makes a face.

That seems about right. Food made before the Revision, when the pills were already in circulation, was always long-endurance and mostly flavorless, in order to promote the idea that it was unnecessary. She puts it in her mouth, and her tongue explodes with warmth and spices and... *taste*. She closes her eyes and a moan escapes her.

"Enjoying yourself?" a voice above her head says, mockingly.

She opens her eyes to find Felix's face inches

from hers. His chin is covered with a short stubble, and his eyes look half-closed and puffy.

She offers him a biscuit and, after looking at it for a split second, he stuffs it in his mouth, devouring it in two bites.

"Wait, you need to taste..." she starts to say, but it's already gone. Wordlessly, she puts another in his palm. And another, and another, until the packet is empty.

She falls to watching him, amused.

"Better?" she asks.

"Nope."

"Why don't you just tell me what work you've done so far on the Clock? I mean, I don't see why you or anyone else should give a merc about whether the Clock is ready in time, but... But. That Vis was sort of scary."

"Was it?" He sounds distracted.

"I think it was. Not that I get why you left school to come here in the first place."

"Oh, didn't I explain?" he says. "I guess I didn't. Maybe that's why you don't get it."

He won't tell her.

Oh, who cares?

"So, no progress at all," she says. Ursa gives out a low rumble. "Careful," Astra tells Felix. "Just lean against her lightly, her fur will warm you right up. Trust me, you don't want her getting mad." For once, Felix doesn't say anything smart back, he just obeys her. He leans back against the bear, closing his eyes with a small sigh. His knees stick up as he tries to fold his long legs close to his body for warmth.

"No progress," he admits after a pause. "Except for learning that I may have had a grandfather, so... so what? I wasn't created in a tube?"

"Not everyone is," she replies. "I wasn't."

"Yeah, but you're..." he stops.

"I'm what?" she asks, interested.

He turns to look her straight in the eye. "I have absolutely no idea what you are, match girl," he says.

"Have you... have you searched every room?" Astra asks, looking away. Her throat suddenly feels dry. "Every corner of the palace?"

He scoffs when she calls the old man's home a palace, but it is a palace to her. She's lived most of her life in huts and makeshift trash shacks. A few stolen days every year, whenever they could sneak her out of the Settlements and bring her to the mountains, she spent with her father's band of Rebels. She hardly ever saw him in those days, but she stayed in the caves with the Rebels; she learned how to survive with them. No, she learned how to *live*. Then she lived in the Box -if you call that living, which you don't- and after that in the snowy planes of the Arctic. She lived in a hole in the ice for a few hours, which were very nearly her last hours, and the ice shack is better than them all.

Felix shrugs. "I've looked," he says.

"Did you find this key?" she lifts it, dangling it in front of his eyes. Not that he knows what a key is for, probably.

She found it in the tin box with the matches, under the plastic biscuit container. Felix grabs it from her fingers. His own long ones are shaking. His hair is curling at the nape of his neck, matted with melting snowflakes, the black stripe at the front getting white with snow. His eyelashes, too. His lips are turning blue.

He keeps looking at the key as though he expects it to start talking to him.

"What does it open?" Astra asks him, beginning to get up on legs stiff from the cold. The snowflakes twirl all around her and she can't help herself. She buries her hand in the snow, picking up a fluffy handful of white frothy coldness. She presses it between her icy-cold fingers until it becomes hard enough, and then she flings it to the sky. It bursts into a million pieces, showering her with soft shards of ice. She squeals in happiness.

She opens her mouth and a snowflake lands on her tongue. She lets it melt there, deliciously, thinking that this must be the taste of freedom.

"Have you got the plague, match girl?" Felix asks behind her. "You're going crazy, aren't you?"

She ignores him, opening the green door and walking inside, shaking the snow from her hair.

sixteen

tin soldier

The match girl showers him with a torrent of snowflakes as she twirls about, flinging her long hair this way and that.

They're inside again.

She's lost what little mind she had, he's sure of it.

"All right, let's start," she says. How does she have the energy to get on all fours and start knocking her fingers on the floor-boards like a lunatic? He feels ready to drop to his knees from exhaustion. "Can you hold this? I need to free it."

She's lifted the red timer carpet which looks like something the little kids make down in the Persian Coast and is trying to roll it away from the floor.

"A pink-and-black pill, that's what you need," he says. "Maybe two."

She turns those merking eyes on him, all silent and pleading. A few seconds later, he's on his knees, helping her. The floor is bare from corner to corner in a minute, and she taps away on the floorboards until he feels his head will burst.

After five minutes of pure torture, a tap sounds different than all the rest.

She taps her knuckles again, just to check, and he crawls quickly to get next to her. Finally he gets what she's doing. There's a small opening in the board, and she pushes the key into it. It turns with a click. Together, they pry the board off.

Beneath it, there's a hole. A vacant rectangular space yawns below the floor.

A hiding place.

Felix feels lightheaded at the discovery.

It was that simple this whole time? Why didn't he think to look on the stupid floorboards? Maybe because he's normal? Then again, what has been normal about this whole thing from the start? Of course, he didn't know floors had boards until now, but he should have thought of it.

He hears a dull thud next to him, and turns around quickly. Astra is crumpled on the floor, her head flopped to the side, boneless, the flames of her hair spread out all around her.

Her face is white.

Felix grabs her shoulder. "Hey," he says quietly, then repeats it more loudly. Is this what sleep looks like? It looks far too much like death, or like a soldier in his regiment that had been wounded so severely no pill could fix him. They had to take him to the Infirmary before he could wake up.

Astra opens her eyes with a little choking sound, then sits slowly up and coughs. "Sorry," she says. "It happens sometimes to me -when I haven't been eating." She bends low, putting her head between her knees.

Felix swallows. He knows what she's talking about. That was no sleep.

Astra lets out a laugh, no doubt seeing the expression on his face, then gathers her curls in one hand and away from her face. It's starting to get some color back -he likes it much better this way. Not that he likes it at all, that is he doesn't exactly ha-...

"In the Old Times, you know," she tells him, "the man was supposed to go out and bring food for the women and children. Not that I mind getting it for myself, but it's pitch-black outside by now, and Ursa won't need to feed for a few more hours. Just saying, that's how it was then..."

"Well, this isn't the merking Old Times, is it?" Felix hears himself yelling, but he can't seem to stop. He's never yelled so much in his life. His ears are beginning to hurt from the sound of his own frustration. "We've left those timers behind forever. Everything is perfect."

This is one of the Chairman's quotes.

He doesn't know how it slipped out of his mouth before he had time to think of it. But, then again, it's true, so what?

"Perfect, huh?" Astra mimics him, cocking her

head like a question mark. "Then why is your stomach hurting with hunger right now? Why can't Ursa find anything but tiny old fish to eat?"

I don't know! He wants to yell, but he's done with yelling for today. Besides, she's already getting up on shaky legs, swaying so much that he has to steady her with a hand across her shoulders, and puts her foot in the hole on the ground.

"What...?" Oh. He can just about discern the first step glowing faintly in the light of the room. There's a staircase beneath the floor. "Hold on, I'll better go in first," he tells her, pushing her aside not gently, but not with as much force as he would have used right after that 'the man has to bring the food' remark either. "Sorry for eating all the biscuits," he murmurs under his breath as he takes the stairs two at a time, hoping she won't hear.

"I'd have given them to you anyway," she replies, right on his heels. "You needed them more. Sorry for calling you a wimp before."

"You're not sorry at all," he replies, but he feels a grin spreading across his face. Good thing it's dark as a colonel's boot down here and there's no way she can see. "Where's a match now, match girl? We sure could use a little light."

She doesn't answer -he knows they have to save them all. Just think, a tiny little stick saved his life. There might be some truth in this Old

Times malarkey she's spewing. He feels with his foot for the next step. Astra stumbles behind him, and his arm shots out in reflex to keep her from falling. "Mind your step," he tells her.

This he can do. Light or dark, scouting is one of the things he knows best.

They descend the stairs until it gets so cold their noses feel like they're going to fall off. Finally, the ground turns flat. "Don't move," he says, his voice laced with authority.

He spreads his arms out carefully until his hands meet the wall. He runs his fingers over its cool, sleek surface, and in a second they meet a metallic slab. Here we are. He walks carefully closer and gently passes his hand in front of it. The next second, the whole place is flooded in light.

Behind him Astra gives out a loud gasp and flops down on the lowest step, as though her legs have given way.

He's next to her in one long stride. "Do you need to lie down again?" Her weakness should annoy him, but instead he feels worried. It's making him mad -more at himself than her.

But her eyes are wide open, her mouth a perfect circle of surprise. Then she licks her lips, and although he knows they have discovered an entire universe down here, Felix can't take his eyes off them, for some stupid reason.

"Wooooow," Astra says, sounding

approximately two years old.

He starts to ask her if she's finally lost it, but just then a loud noise makes him jump. The next second he's gotten down, his body laid out flat on the ground. Without thinking, he drags Astra beneath him, his hand moving to cover her head. A loud, banging sound is bursting around them, echoing rapidly like shots from timer weapons, coming from everywhere, piercing his eardrums.

Her head tucked nicely in his chest, Astra starts mumbling something.

"Be quiet," he hisses.

What on mars is this place? Is it a land mine or something? The sound of weapons is deafening, but it's beginning to repeat itself. Maybe it's some kind of Vis, prerecorded, that activates as soon as someone steps down here, meant to frighten intruders.

Before he has time to lift his head carefully to investigate, the voice starts.

"So, my boy, you found yourself down here."

It's Ulysses.

seventeen

match girl

When the lights came on, Astra thought her eyes would pop out of her head. She's never seen anything like this before.

She thought the shack was a palace, but this... this is heaven.

There aren't any rooms down here, just an endless arcade -it seems endless to her eyes, but it isn't, of course. There's a huge arch above her head, dark brown, as if it's made of wood, although probably it's some kind of a synthetic alternative, and below it begins a narrow passageway that leads on in a straight line. To the left and right great openings appear beneath stark white arches, made of pristine cast. But that's where the white ends.

The arches are glowing with fluorescent light, hidden below their curves, and the entire hall is tinted in a light-bluish white.

Just peeking inside the openings left and right of the arcade's narrow passageway, she can see all sorts of strange objects, bathed in the artificial arch light. There's timer stuff and ancient objects, strange, unknown, as far as the eye can see. Most of them are thin and flat, lined up in colorful shelves. She knows what they are; at least she thinks she does. They're the most dangerous weapons, and none are supposed to have survived the Revision. But the Rebels had a couple of them, caked in the mud of decades and half-burned -they'd been salvaged from the Revision burnings- still she's fairly certain that's what they were.

Books.

"Oh," she gasps.

In here there are thousands of them. A room full of weaponry -illegal weaponry. There was no mention in the Vis of the old man wanting Felix to start a war. Then again, if he was preparing a revolution in the merking basement of his ice shack, he wouldn't say that in a Vis, for any hacker to stumble upon, would he?

"Wooooow"

It comes out of her lips before her brain has time to realize what her mouth is saying. She has to sit down, because she feels dizzy, but this time it isn't from lack of food. The tin soldier next to her has no idea of course, what he's seeing.

And then the music starts and all hell breaks loose.

Out of nowhere, Felix grabs her and pushes her on the floor, covering her head with his elbow, shielding her with his body. What does he think it is?

She supposes that he may never have heard music before. Her heart constricts with a sadness so overpowering at this realization that she can think of nothing else. She feels a hollowness at the pit of her stomach, her eyes stinging with tears.

They certainly don't let soldiers-in-training listen to music. And she doubts that those apartments in New Baghdad that they stick five boys in and a Mother-droid to 'take care' of them have much use for it either. He can't have experienced anything like the singing that drifts to the skies from the women workers' lines as they go about picking up fruit and feeding animals in the Farms.

"So, my boy, you found yourself down here," the old man's voice surprises her. "Like the sound of that music? Thought it might get your attention -then again, they might have swept music from your brain along with everything good, those bastards."

She leaps to her feet, since Felix seems to have frozen on the spot, but that has its good side, because he finally removed his hand from around her. She starts running down the arcade, her teeth chattering with cold, her steps echoing on the soft floor underneath the white, glowing arches.

"Astra, wait!" Felix's voice yells at her from behind.

She knows what he's thinking. It could be a trap, it could be a Projection, a Hologram, anything. It could even be the old man come back from the dead to haunt them.

"You're sweet, but I'm fine," she yells back at him. She knows the 'sweet' part will infuriate him, maybe more than the time she called him a coward. She's right. In a second, his steps are echoing loudly behind her, his boots slapping the floor as he runs to her.

"It's just a Vis," she tells him as soon as he reaches her, panting.

They're facing the wall at the end of the hall, where a thin, floor-length PR screen is installed. The face of Ulysses, exactly the same as in the other Vis, stares back at them, his eyebrows drawn together, his lips thin, his eyes fierce.

'I hope it didn't take you too long to discover the floor board,' Ulysses says in the Vis, then he leans down and his bushy eyebrows fill the screen. 'On the other hand, you may never make your way down here. Those machine Mothers, that joke of a military school... they do more to keep you stupid and blind to your surroundings than train you into manhood and... humanness.' Ulysses swallows, obviously trying to get himself under control. A vein has appeared on his forehead and is throbbing with bottled-up anger.

'Heart silent as a stone still, is it?' he goes on, letting out a harsh little laugh. 'Or are you finally getting mad at something? Perhaps the fact that I pulled you from your elite school? Or maybe dropping the bomb on you that your parents aren't a cold slab in a lab, but actual persons? Your father is my son, and thus I'm your grandfather. I'm not even sure you know how it works, the whole parents thing...'

And then something happens that manages to surprise Astra.

There's not much that can do that these days.

But when Felix wordlessly passes a palm in front of the PR and freezes it mid-sentence, turning his back on the old man's face and walking away slowly, as though every step requires more effort than he can muster, she's completely thrown.

"Come on," he says to her, like he can sense her standing there confused. "I've had enough."

So they walk up the steps and replace the floorboard.

Felix walks on and flings himself beside the heater. Astra thinks he's overreacting a bit, even though she realizes that his world is in the process of being torn to pieces.

Still, she can't help herself.

"People used to say 'goodnight' before they went to sleep in the- before it became obsolete," she says.

"Did they used to say 'go to Mercury'?" his voice sounds muffled. He's already half asleep.

"Humans hadn't landed on Mercury back then," she replies, feeling the sadness descend again. "That is they had; but it hadn't been colonized yet."

There's a short silence, and she thinks he's fallen asleep.

"I'm going back tomorrow," he murmurs crossly. "Put on my Hydro jacket, would you? You're shaking so bad, it's getting on my nerves." He pauses for a second, and his breath sounds even, regular. Peaceful. "That's an order, match girl. An order from the Chairman's Inter... Interglatic Armaries lieute-"

His voice fades away and Astra, smiling, gets up to go put his jacket on. Immediately her body starts to warm itself deliciously. His scent, a combination of soap, sweat and boyhood, still lingers on the rubbery material, but it's almost faded so that it hardly bothers her.

She feels a sudden surge of heat on her cheeks, as the remembers the feel of his hard, lean body on top of hers when he fell on her, trying to protect her from the music's imaginary gunshots. She remembers how his breath stirred the hair behind her ear, how his arms felt, wrapped tight around hers.

It makes her shudder just to think of how close their bodies were. She passes a hand through her hair, slowly running it all the way down through the tangles. She'll have to take care that something like *that* never happens again.

Shivering, she hugs the jacket closer to her body. The smile spreads again on her face.

She'd been waiting for the soldier to start thinking of someone other than himself. It's not his fault that he wasn't taught this, but she was beginning to think he was a tin soldier through and through.

The verdict is still up on that.

But maybe that's what that thing he did back at the staircase was. Thinking of somebody else and not just of himself –trying to protect her first, putting his body between her and the danger.

It was a good thing he did.

Misguided, but good.

She wraps the jacket more tightly about her - it's swimming on her, but still it does its job, which is to keep her from freezing- and lays down in the other room. Let him have his privacy. Tomorrow he's going back to school, he says.

We'll see.

Astra falls asleep laughing softly to herself.

She hadn't smiled in years. It's a nice change.

eighteen

match girl

As Astra lies there, huddled in the soldier's Hydro military jacket on the Clockmaster's ice shack floor, the snow pouring silently outside the window, something insubstantial slithers underneath the green door, something ugly and cruel, darker than the blackest smoke. It begins weaving its tendrils around her sleeping head, soundlessly, until it wraps her entire body in its ethereal fingers.

In a split second, Astra finds herself in a room larger than the lake which almost swallowed her alive, standing in a space almost exactly the width of her feet. Next to her there's a woman, about fifty years old. She, too, is standing. The entire room is filled with standing women, hundreds, maybe thousands of them. Each one doesn't have more space to stand in than her own body's width. Once every two days they are given pills to keep them awake, to keep them from dropping from hunger.

And that's it.

This is the Box -the women's version of it.

It's night outside the prison by Astra's calculations, although there are no windows here of course, and she hasn't seen the sky in eighteen months. So it may very well be noon outside the prison, the sun streaming down on the Appalachian mountains.

Inside, a woman starts to howl.

"Single file from the left," a guard barks. "And don't take forever."

They can't form lines standing like that, with scarcely room enough to breathe between them. So the guard's order can only mean one thing. They're letting them out. There's going to be another execution.

Women Felons are executed within two months of entering the Box, or if they are underage, on the day of their sixteenth birthday. Astra's sixteenth birthday won't be for another good eight months or so, but she knows they won't hang her. They probably have a much more painful death prepared for the daughter of Christopher Steadfast. And much less public.

The Terrestrial Channel is supposed to broadcast every execution for the purposes of transparency, according to Chairman Kun, but no one ever watches them anymore -they have no interest whatsoever.

They won't show her own execution. They won't risk anyone even remembering her father and maybe getting ideas. She knows that as well as she knows exactly how many hours she's been standing on the same narrow tile inside the Box. She's counted every one of them. Today it's a girl about Astra's age who will be murdered.

It is night after all, slightly earlier than Astra had calculated, but still pretty close. The sky is a canopy of black velvet and as soon as the guards give them the signal to stop walking, Astra turns her eyes upwards and tries to separate the stars from the satellites. It smells like earth and metal and blood out here.

Astra can't count very well -it's illegal for a woman to learn at all, unless she's in the Elite circles, of course. The Rebels, among other things, started teaching her to count to a hundred. Then her father was arrested and she was put in the Box, so there was no more time for lessons.

"The stars are the least shiny of all the points in the heaven," Matt used to say, while he was working. She remembers him always fiddling with something in his calloused hands: tying two long sticks together to make a bow, a fishing pole, or scribbling down on a paper. "Also, their positions are random. Take the Ursa Major constellation, for example. You can see that its three stars are apart just enough so that, just by holding your thumb like this you can-"

"You there!" a harsh voice snaps her back to

reality. "Eyes on the wall."

They have to watch.

It's mandatory.

They have to watch as every inmate in turn is hung by the neck, day after day. They have to watch the terror in their eyes, they have to taste death on their own lips before their time comes, they have to be aware of what's in store for them.

Just by watching, Astra feels her own throat close up. She's suffocating, her heart beating like a drum. Her temples are screaming, throbbing in her head. And that's not even the worst part.

You can't rest your eyes for a second; you'd be stupid to relax for less. The stories keep circulating, new ones added every week, of a girl who fell asleep standing up, and woke again in the Guards' quarters, being ripped apart - literally- as they each took their turn with her. Her body was just thrown away with the executed after they were done.

Hundreds, thousands of stories like that -so many that the girls have stopped noticing. Even worse are the Harvests. These happen regularly, every week or so, in the Box.

They just lead the women in formation inside the labs and take their eggs. For two years, Astra was reaped dry. She still expects them to come whenever she shuts her eyes. It's become part of her, a vile, horrific part, but right now there's nowhere to run when they come in her sleep, and yell at her to line in and shut up.

She wakes up to screams. She doesn't panic,
because this isn't the first time she's woken up to
screaming -or worse. She merely opens her eyes
to assess the seriousness of the threat.\The first
thing she sees is an open mouth, teeth glistening
as it shouts curses at her.

"What?" she squints into Felix's frantic eyes.

"Nothing," he replies, clearing his throat as he
gets up. "You were... making weird noises in your
sleep."

Astra sits up, pretending to yawn, but she's
actually shaking pretty badly. The room is dark -
Felix must have closed the shutters on the
windows again. What is it with the soldier and
closed spaces? Her throat feels hoarse as though
she's been screaming, her tongue dry. It was the
dream again. It followed her all the way up here.
She can't escape the memories, not even in her
sleep.

"It's..." she needs to clear her throat. "Sorry. I
was suffocating." Oh, merc. She didn't mean to
tell him that.

"I saw," Felix replies.

His eyes are shining with some emotion -
contempt perhaps? His eyebrows are furrowed
down so low, his forehead is full of wrinkles. He
looks away quickly. She doesn't know why this
bothers her, because it shouldn't, but it does. "I

don't suppose you know what dreams, that is... what nightmares are?"

Felix doesn't reply for a second. He strides to the window, opening the blinds and stares intently outside. That's new.

"I'm starting to find out," he says finally, not turning to look at her. "I woke up to giant clock chasing me into a hole of ice water, and I was swimming as fast as I could to get away from it, but then Ulysses or someone who looked freakishly like him blocked my way -I was somehow back in school by this time, and then he said in my Colonel's voice to 'form a single file and shut up' and that's when I woke up to find it was you who'd yelled the order."

Astra has stood up and is arranging the cloak around her, raking her fingers through her wild locks to try to tame them. "You can swim?" is all she asks.

"Not for much longer," he replies. "It looks like I might be actually dying from hunger."

"Don't be ridiculous. It would take you at least a month to die from hunger -and that's supposing that your heart beat like an actual human being's, which it doesn't, so you're looking to even longer..."

"Would you shut *up* for one second?" Felix bursts out.

"I stayed in the Box for about two years, that's where the nightmares come from," she says quietly, starting to take his jacket off.

"No, keep it," he says absently, his back to her still.

"Aren't you going back to school today?" she asks, watching him, trying not to smile. His ears turn red, and then the blush starts to spread on the back of his neck. "That's what you said last night, remember? You..."

"I don't see Ursa anywhere," he says.

"She must have wandered off," Astra replies. "She's not our pet after all. She's a wild animal, not that you'd know what that even means." Felix stays silent, his body perfectly still, not moving a finger. "You could go fishing yourself, couldn't you?" she adds softly in a moment. "Just do what Ursa did. Stand above the hole and wait. That's all."

Silence. Then, "And what if I see a... a fish?"

"Then you grab it and pull it out," she says. "Shoot it, if you have to."

For the first time he turns around and fixes those blue eyes on hers. She sucks in a sharp breath, her mind emptying of all thoughts except one. He's lost, she thinks. More so than he knows. More so than me.

"And put your Hydro suit on," she says, trying to make her voice sound normal. "It's going to be a long walk. Try not to get yourself lost."

He's already pulling the Hydro pants on, on top of his cotton ones. "Try to be here when I get back," he tells her. "The shack as well. Don't do anything stupid, like you're always doing. Although I doubt you can help yourself."

"Oh, you can bet your tin little heart I'll do something stupid," Astra murmurs to herself as soon as Felix closes the door behind him with a mighty bang. She falls to her knees and scrambles for the loose floorboard.

n i n e t e e n

t i n   s o l d i e r

He'll die before admitting it, even to himself,
but Felix's mouth is watering. He can't believe
he's actually thinking of the weird, frothy taste of
the fish-thingy he ate yesterday. The truth is,
right now, if one offered him the choice between
all the riches of the Chairman and one more bite
of that food, he'd take the bite.

That's just absurd.

His steps are taking him forward, of their own
will, his brain automatically following the exact
path the bear took yesterday, although by now it's
been covered several times over by snow -he has a
photographic memory, very useful for the
military.

His nostrils flare as his muscles warm up by
the exercise. His eyes are stinging from the cold.
At least his legs are warm. The kind of stupidity
that made him leave his jacket to the match girl
would be punished severely by his General.

Strange thing is, as he was standing there,
taking in her white cheeks and thin wrists, from

the corner of his eye, he felt as though he had no choice but to let her wear it.

As he has no choice but to press on, trudging through the knee-deep snow. right now.

'Are you in a gang?' he remembers her asking just as he'd lifted her out of the hole in the ice. He'd wondered what she meant, if she'd lost her mind. Then he thinks of how he found her last night, how broken she sounded in her sleep, when she was in the grip of that thing... nightmare she called it. He swallows hard.

He's heard of the Harvests that take place in the women's Box, but he always thought the tales had gotten grossly exaggerated in the telling. He's heard of the 'Raper gangs', a play on the word 'Reaper', which is slang for the Harvesters. He's not sure what it means.

Well, he wasn't sure until last night.

Now he's got a pretty good idea of the kind of horrifying experience Astra must have been re-living in her sleep. And when she first opened her eyes and saw him, back at the frozen lake, she must have seen his uniform and thought that he... That he... He can't catch his breath.

Get your head in the battle, lieutenant! His General's voice shouts in his head.

Yes, the battle. This is just one more battle he must win. Only he's never fought against hunger, against weakness... against a merking nightmare before. He's never been trained for any of these.

It's all the old man's fault.

"You old timer ruined my life!" Felix yells into the whiteness like a madman.

It feels good, somehow.

So he yells it again, adding in a few curses for good measure. He yells it until the silence echoes with it, until his neck is roped with thick veins, his breath coming short.

But his heart stays as still as ever.

He falls to his knees, feeling like a stupid two-year-old boy, and lifts his eyes to the heavens.

The sky is infinitely blue, dusted with a few clouds here and there, the trees marking the dark line of the horizon ahead.

Without warning, Astra's exclamation from last night pops into his head. "Wooooooow," he whispers.

It doesn't enter his mind right then that he's been robbed of all of this, of beauty, of life, of the very world for seventeen years. It will in a few moments, when he gets up, his hair crusted with snow -not that he'll notice- and makes straight for the trees.

And then he'll get angry.

He'll kick up a storm of snow as he walks.

He'll curse some more, feeling his eyes sting with the tears of a million unasked questions.

When he returns to the shack, a few hours later, all red-cheeked and blood-smeared, a precious bundle in his hands, it hits him for the first time.

Astra isn't just the first girl he's ever met. She's the first female human being. The 'Mother' he grew up with wasn't human, although he didn't know it at the time. She was an android. He learnt all about how women and men have to be separate in the One World, if any form of peace is to be sustained. But the boys have to be raised by someone before they'll be grown up enough to undertake professions. So the 'Mothers' were created.

Sweet and gentle, perfect for performing simple tasks and keeping the boys alive, but nothing more than that. He'd thought she was a bit stupid when he first got out of the Box, seeing as the boys spent their time in their private PRs, educating themselves with no help from her, except being told what time it was and how they should spend the next hour according to their daily timetable -which was issued by the Ministry of Education.

Felix is by no means as intelligent as he thought he was, these last days have made it plainly obvious, and if they hadn't, the match girl has told him so times enough, but he isn't stupid.

Which is why his brain immediately jumps to the next question.

Who else in his life isn't what they told him he was? Who else has lied to him?

He was taught, among every other boy in New Baghdad, that contacting a person of the opposite sex would infect him with diseases, possibly the After Plague, since they -the women and girls- lived in the Islands, in very different conditions than them, and carried different germs.

It was all lies.

The same thing that nearly killed Astra had nearly killed him as well that first night. They feel the same hunger, very nearly have the same thoughts. Sure, she irritates the merc out of him, and probably she thinks the same of him, but apart from that she is no threat. She's no contamination.

She is, mostly, no different than him.

As he opens the green door he's debating whether to talk about this with her -she's after all made it plainly clear that she knows *everything*- and then he stops short.

The shack is empty and freezing.

Felix flings the things he was carrying to the floor and almost jumps through the loose floorboard. 'Try not to do anything stupid,' he told her. Turns out he was the stupid one for trusting her.

"Astra!" he calls. "Match girl, where the timers are you?"

He almost wishes her in Mars. The entire place downstairs is flooded in light, the arches glowing with it, as it's pouring down from some source behind the woodwork. It's also incredibly warm in here. Perhaps the old man had some sort of fancy wall-heating system like the Chairman's mansion and some of the Elite's residences are rumored to have.

Whatever it is, it's making his cheeks burn with heat.

"Astra!" he yells again, hearing something ugly in his voice.

He doesn't like it.

"In here," her voice answers. About time, too.

He jogs towards it, and then his jaw drops to the ground. Well, almost.

She's seated on the carpet, inside one of the arches, tiny red, blue and green lights blinking like eyes all around her. There's a million clocks in the room, small, tiny ones, some a bit bigger, but nothing to even compare with the size of the Clock. There's carved leaves on them and birds and other animals carved in wood, some people with timer clothes and colors. Most of the clocks have little windows and tiny doors, as though something is expected to come out of them. There's metal pine cones and arrows hanging from a long chain underneath many of them. One little clock is identical to the ice shack, its tilted roof covered in fake snow, with a little green door at the front, curtains at the windows. Then there's a red bird-house, with weird pointy-shaped leaves carved all around it, a timer school, a timer clock-tower and other boring animal likenesses. There's so much color in here it's hurting his eyes.

In a little empty space, next to the clocks, a tiny PR screen is attached to the wall, and Astra has turned it on, and flicked to an open fire, which crackles loudly, its flames competing with the color of her hair.

What is it with this girl and flames?

The wall opposite him is filled with books, all sizes -most of them thicker than his thumb- and Astra, still wrapped in his jacket, is sitting cross-legged on the floor, her hair tamed in a long braid, with one of the books open in her lap.

She's taken off the cloak -thankfully- and underneath the jacket she's wearing strange timer clothes that are several sizes too big for her, or they were, because she appears to have stitched a pair of pants together at the seams so that they fit her perfectly. Did these belong to the Clockmaster? The design certainly looks old timer, low-waist and fitted all the way to her ankles, but the fabric can't be older than two years. They don't look horrible on her, at least; they look almost decent. They look...

Felix quickly tears his eyes away.

The little lights are reflected off Astra's hair, giving them a blue, green and yellow color alternatively. It's sort of cool. That is, it's sort of cool until he realizes that everything inside the arch -including himself- is giving off the color of the lights as they change continuously, ad nauseam. Even the book in her fingers.

"What do you think you're doing with that?" he asks her in a clipped voice. That's what he needs right now. Another felony to add to her -and his- crimes.

Astra slowly lifts her eyes to his face. "Not reading it, that's for sure," she says quietly.

Felix's head drops between his shoulders. He studies his shoes. Of course. She can't read. He knew that; in fact he knows why women aren't allowed to read: for one thing, they don't need it. And for another, women used to cause a great deal of trouble in the Old Times, getting weird and subversive ideas, no need to repeat the mistakes of the past.

Then why are his eyes stinging with tears for the second time today?

Why does it feel like it's the greatest felony of all, the biggest crime in the Planet, that this smart, animated little person who's managed to keep herself as well as him alive for days, isn't able to put letters together to read a simple phrase? She's Steadfast's daughter, for merc's sake. Steadfast might have been a criminal, but he was also a genius. And now this girl, his only reason for holding onto life as long as he did, while electricity was being poured into his body, is reduced to living like a droid, or worse, like a...

like a woman.

That's not right, Felix knows that with absolute conviction.

He sniffles loudly, then brings the back of his hand to his mouth. Great, now she knows he's weak -well, it isn't as though she didn't know before.

"No luck, huh?" she murmurs, looking him up and down, taking in his snow-crusted boots, melting in a pool by his feet, and his empty hands pointedly.

And just like that, his compassion is gone.

"No luck, no," he answers her lightly. "Just hours and hours of stalking and freezing and having the best aim in the regiment."

"You ate it all, then," she concludes.

"No, you idiot, it's upstairs."

"What is?"

With a long-suffering sigh, he flops to the ground, stretching his legs in front of him, feeling the warmth of the basement's inner-heating system seep through the floor into his limbs. "Let's see," he begins, counting on his fingers. "First there was a small furry animal, which gave me a merc of a time, it was so fast, but I followed it through the trees until it stood still, and then..."

"And then?" Astra has put the book aside and is watching him with a weird expression on her face. He's got the strange idea that this is some sort of test.

"And then I aimed to shoot it, but I... didn't want to," he says. "For one, this is the first time I've seen... I've seen..."

"You've seen an animal different than yourself," she finishes. "Except for me, of course."

"Of course." She's made him smile again, the match girl. "For another, it didn't look as though it would be... pleasant to eat. Anyway, I grabbed a handful of what it was eating, some sort of plant, but hard and round... you'll see."

"Nuts," she says.

"I haven't got a clue. Then I walked all the way to Ursa's hole and waited and..." He lets his voice trail dramatically. It occurs to him that he hasn't felt so proud in his entire life as he does at this moment.

Astra's entire face lights up. "You caught one?"

He lifts his left eyebrow. "Nope," he says, and her face falls a little, but she tries not to show it. "Three."

Before he knows what's happening, there's a squeal and then his arms are full of Astra. She flings herself to him, her arms closing around his waist, her hair reaching just below his jaw.

Then, just as quickly, she leaves him alone.

"Thank you," she whispers, lifting her dark eyes to his. "Now, for what *I* found."

She looks so smug, he hasn't got the heart to tell her that he thinks she's probably found something that will turn his world around again and thanks, but he's not interested. Besides, he's still got the breath knocked out of him after what she did.

"Go into the hall, and take a left into the second arch." Astra's eyes are positively sparkling. Oh, what the merc.

He goes into the hall, then turns left as she told him to.

And he was right.

His world is turned upside down once more.

t w e n t y

t i n   s o l d i e r

Inside the arch it's like a small empty room without a door. It's three white walls, glowing with a pale yellow light, and nothing much else. No tiny lights, no clocks lining the ceiling, no giant bookshelf filled with illegal books and timer knick-knacks, like the other arches. This one is basically empty, there's nothing here.

Except for the Clock.

It stands -no, it floats- a few centimeters off the floor, in a vertical position, just a round bronze frame twice Felix's height, with cogwheels and gears hanging every which way out of its huge belly.

Ulysses must have started to paint the Latin numbers on, just big, plain lines, and that's all the work he's done. The back of the clock is a jumble of wires and little counting screens, but Felix knows that these will have to be fully concealed before the Clock is ready for the Perennial. It will have to stand alone, no connection to a power source, or anything nanotech related. Mostly it has to work mechanically, with something called a gear system, and if some sort of newer tech has to be employed, so that the 'spectacle the Clockmaster provides for the Chairman's guests is on par with their refined tastes' -Ulysses' words, not his- it has to be absolutely invisible. It isn't yet, this much Felix can see.

And that's as far as his knowledge goes.

"Is this amazing or what?" Astra says behind him.

He has the sudden urge to bang his head against the wall.

"'Dead' is the word I was going for," he says absently. "As in, we'll be dead in a few days."

Astra shrugs. "I'm dead already, for them," is all she says. "Come on, I'm starving."

They don't go upstairs again, except to fetch the fish and acorns, and the heater. Astra plops herself on the carpet below the red and blue lights again, claiming this is 'her corner' and that 'it's pretty and warm down here, don't you think?' which he doesn't -think, that is- and starts charring the stars out of his fish.

They eat, and he can barely keep his mouth from moaning in pleasure like hers. It didn't taste like this yesterday, did it? This is the best thing that's ever existed. It melts across his tongue, exploding in taste, and for a moment he can barely resist making the same weird noises Astra was producing yesterday. Then they proceed to break their teeth on the acorns, and after that's done, Astra looks him up and down -again- and murmurs something unintelligible.

"Do you have something to say to me?" he asks her.

"Lots," she says, giving him a smile full of teeth. "But what I just said was 'brainless Drone'."

"A brainless Drone who just fed you," he retorts.

"I said thank you, didn't I?" she says quickly, and then changes the subject. "Will you read something to me?"

They're seated with their backs against the books, since there is no wall free of them in here, and Felix has flung his head back, staring at the ceiling, and licking his fingers shamelessly. At her words, he sits up straight.

"We'll see," he says, but it comes out all choked up, as though he's been trying not to scream for the past half hour.

Astra doesn't seem to notice.

She lifts her arm and points to the crown of arch. "There," she says. "Aren't these words?"

"Just one," Felix says, standing up and beginning to pick up their plates. "Christmas."

Astra nods, although the word must be as foreign to her as it is to him. "Leave these, I'll take care of them," she says. "And while I do, would you go around and read what the arches say? Most of them, at least."

He's already out in the hall before she's finished talking.

He knows she's going to have to climb the stairs in order to wash their plates, but still he starts yelling the words he finds, hoping she's still there to listen to them.

His boots slap the floor as he steps in and out of the arches quickly, reading the names -there are so many of them, he's got to be quick.

"Romans," he yells, getting into the first arch to his left. The three-walled room is filled with a great, useless pile of metal swords and other weird-shaped, obsolete objects. Family, another sign says on an arch's crown.

Felix walks on, calling names as he reads them, trying not to peek too much inside the different compartments, because he could be here all day.

Nature and Biology, he reads. Newton, says another, I don't know what that means. First Enlightenment, there's a little word beside it, it's hard to read... Oh, it says 'the real one'. Music - Astra squeals at that, good, she's still here. Food. Battles. Sickness. Houses and Dwellings. Survival, Africa. Games -this one is a mess. Art. Art 2, Art 3... it goes on for ten arches like that. The New Europe and Asia -Europea. Comfort and Beauty. Twenty-five, Twenty-five, that's what it says above the Clock.

Then Felix stops talking.

He stops running too, his chest rising and falling unevenly -and it's not from running.

"Are you there?" Astra asks in a moment. "Soldier?" Her voice gets louder, squeakier, but even if he wanted to talk to her, just to say that he's ok, he couldn't.

He hears her steps approaching hurriedly behind him in a second. "What's wrong?" she asks as she reaches him, out of breath. He feels her hand on his elbow. He's become a statue, he can't move, he can't breathe, he can't think.

"Hey, sit down before you fall over," Astra's voice brings him back to reality. He falls to his knees. "I said sit down, but ok. Come on, breathe. What's this one? What does it say?"

It takes three efforts to get it out.

When it finally does, the match girl finally shuts up. He wishes he hadn't. Her voice was the only thing anchoring him to reality, to sanity.

Astra walks around the room.

It's full of shelves, too, and some of them have boxes on them. The rest are filled with books, but they're not timer books. He can tell from their spines: they're journals, hand-written, volumes and volumes of them.

"Felix," Felix says in a hoarse voice. "It has my name on it."

She leaves him alone after that, and they spend the entire day below, but he doesn't see her until much later, when his stomach feels hollow with hunger again, and he can't go outside to hunt, because the plains are pitch black with night.

He doesn't know what she does all day. Felix doesn't even know what *he* does all day. All he knows is that the night finds him on the warm floor, seated right below the arch, his muscles tingling with immobility.

He hasn't touched a thing, not the journals, or the boxes. Not the little portable PR screen with the earplugs on the old desk in the corner.

"Are you done?" Astra's voice asks him from a few paces away. She's never sounded scared before, nor does she now, but there's a weird hesitation in her voice that bothers him for some stupid reason.

He can't hear her steps approaching, and it almost makes him smile to know that she's hesitating -for once- before getting in his face. "Come in," he tells her.

He sees that her eyes have grown huge and even darker since he last saw them. They're also puffy and red, but she doesn't look sad; she looks mad. "Have you read any of the... weapons?" she asks him sullenly and he stops himself just a second before he bursts into laughter.

She's clutching one of the 'weapons' in her hands, a small, dark green hardcover book that looks older than time itself. It can't have more than a hundred pages in it. The edges of the pages look black, and most likely that's because of time and mold -maybe it was rescued from one of the fires of the Revision, although droids know why anyone would go into the trouble of saving it. Books had all but become obsolete by then.

He gets up slowly, his limbs coming to life with pins and needles pricking at his skin, feeling as though he's waking from one of Astra's horrible nightmares.

"We don't call them 'weapons'," he corrects her gently, and although this would be an excellent opportunity for him to take his revenge for being called a 'Drone' and a 'tin soldier' for the better part of two days, right now all he tries to do is to make himself sound less superior, stars know why. "That's what children are told, children and..."

And women, he wants to add. He's spoken 'of children and women' so many times, he's lost count. But this time he can't seem to finish the phrase.

Astra just stands there, fixing him with those stormy eyes. She won't say the word for him. He won't say it either, he decides. "So that they knew it would be dangerous for them to pick them up randomly and read them. Back when there were books lying about; there haven't been since before you were born."

"Obviously there are," Astra says dryly. "And why would it be dangerous?"

He shrugs. "They... well, some of them have ideas inside, and that's the danger."

"Sounds stupid to me," she says, turning her back to him. "I mean, they forbid us to learn how to read and write, so we can't get any... *ideas* from those paper-weapons anyway, can we?" The word 'ideas' sounds like a swearword on her lips. "But that doesn't mean they can stop us from thinking. I mean," she turns around to cast a glance at him, "most of us at least," she adds sadly and there's not even a hint of mocking in her voice now.

Felix knows she's thinking about the Health Discs. "I'm not taking the merking pills any more am I?" he shouts at her suddenly.

She doesn't even flinch.

"No, you're not," she says quietly.

"Good. Now, give me this half-burnt thing you're twisting in your fingers. If we're for Mercury, we might as well add one more crime to the list."

Wordlessly, she hands him the book.

"All right. Now see here, this is 't', then 'h', then 'e'. Don't worry about remembering them right away, we'll go over the alphabet from the beginning. It's just that these three letters make up the most common word in the English language. So, it says 'the...'." He stops, his eyes turning round as discs. "Ah..."

"What?"

"'The Steadfast Soldier'. That's the title," Felix says.

"Let me see."

To his credit, Felix doesn't laugh. Neither does he point out to her that it won't help if she looks at it. He just shows her. Then he opens to the first page, which is blank and shriveled by heat, and then to the second. There, again, is the title, an intricate frame drawn around it, as well as two silhouettes close together.

One is a boy and another obviously a girl, but she's dressed weirdly: she's wearing a short skirt that fans at a sharp angle from her body. The boy has only one leg.

twenty-one

match girl

Astra leans down to look at the page more carefully, but she doesn't know what to make of the images. Is this the 'dangerous idea' one could get from this book, that a man and a woman can stand so close to each other, perhaps even talk to each other as equals? She's been talking to Felix every day since the day before yesterday, and she hasn't gotten any different than what she was. She hasn't got sick, or rebellious -well, no more than she was.

He's changed, it's true, but how is changing from a tin soldier into a human being a bad thing? It might be dangerous though, now that she thinks of it. Good for him.

And what is up with her father's name in the title?

"Do you want to read it?" Felix asks, yawning.

He doesn't say 'do you want me to read it for you' and she comes as close to liking him for it as possible.

"I don't mind," she answers, pretending she's

not bursting to know what the book says, "but I can't stand it in here. This place is creeping me out. Can we go back to the Chramamas arch?"

"Christmas," he corrects her. "At least that's how I think you say it."

"Like *father Christmas'*." Astra nods, forgetting that he doesn't know what she's talking about.

They start walking side by side, shoulders almost touching -the hallway is just wide enough for both of them- and Felix flips the pages past a few obscure illustrations that have blurred together because of the fire and water damage, finding the first chapter. "What the stars does that mean? Christmas," she says.

"I have no idea," Felix replies.

twenty-two

tin soldier

When they reach the arch, half-way down the gallery, the flames are still crackling in the small PR by the wall. Astra has pulled random books off the shelves and piled them on the floor in neat little columns according to color. The girl is obsessed with it. She's dragged a huge chair, probably from the 'Survival' arch or the 'Comfort and Beauty' which both are more than twenty feet away. The chair takes up the entire corner next to the PR that has this Vis of a fire going on, and she's draped more colors on it, blankets and pieces of fabrics, making a bird's nest on the drab, threadbare seat.

As soon as they reach the arch, Astra gives two little jumps and flings herself on the chair, practically sinking an inch inside its cushions. She almost disappears within it -she's so small there's room for two more persons next to her. The tiny lights are still blinking overhead, the clocks with the little doors reflecting the blue, red and golden glow. He hadn't noticed it before, but there's a merking tree in here. A tree!

The old man had lost his mind, no doubt about it.

The tree, although obviously fake, is so life-like that he looks it twice up and down, just to be certain. It's tall, reaching to the ceiling; almost identical to the firs he walked among this morning, in the woods. He'd never walked beside a tree in his life. He'd fought beside one, he'd trained, crawled, climbed one. But never just looked at it, never smelled it, not really. He's never watched its branches bow with weight under the snow. This tree has no snow on it, although some of its needles are painted white to imitate the look of the frosted pine trees. And of course, it's decorated with silly color-lights just like the bookshelves, its pine needles blinking blue, green and red.

Again with the fire. This girl. Felix shakes his head and sits down, among the piles of books, the lowest branches of the tree scratching his knee. He opens the book.

'There were once,' he starts and then stops to clear his throat. 'There were once five and twenty tin soldiers, who were all brothers, for they had been made out of the same old tin spoon.'

Astra lifts her eyes to meet his, and they stare at each other without talking.

Tin soldier, it said. Five and twenty.

Finally, Astra licks her lips. "What's 'brothers'?" she asks.

"What's a spoon?" Felix asks back.

They haven't taken a pill in two days, and so their bodies need to sleep, but they end up staying awake until dawn. They stumble over foreign words, starting to recognize some of them as the story progresses, and mostly getting more and more confused with each page.

They read about the ballerina who was beautiful -"what does beautiful mean?" asks Astra. They read about the soldier who was steadfast and had lost one leg in the war. "I had a fellow-officer whose leg was blown up," Felix says. "They grew him a new one in four days." They read about the little paper boat, they read about the fish that swallowed the tin soldier, they read about the heart that survived the fire.

They read about the kiss —having no idea what they're reading about.

'They put him on the table,' Felix reads, 'and there he was, back in the same room as before. He saw the same children, the same toys were on the table, and there was the same fine castle with the pretty little dancer. She still balanced on one leg, with the other raised high. She too was steadfast.

'That touched the soldier so deeply that he would have cried tin tears, only soldiers never cry.

'He looked at her, and she looked at him, and never a word was said. Just as things were going so nicely for them, one of the little boys snatched up the tin soldier and threw him into the stove. He did it for no reason at all. That black bogey in the snuffbox must have put him up to it.

'The tin soldier stood there dressed in flames. He felt a terrible heat, but whether it came from the flames or from his love he didn't know. He'd lost his splendid colors, maybe from his hard journey, maybe from grief, nobody can say.

'He looked at the little lady, and she looked at him, and he felt himself melting. But still he stood steadfast, with his musket held trim on his shoulder.

'Then the door blew open.

'A puff of wind struck the dancer. She flew like a sylph, straight into the fire with the soldier, blazed up in a flash, and was gone. The tin soldier melted, all in a lump. The next day, when a servant took up the ashes she found him in the shape of a little tin heart. But of the pretty dancer nothing was left except her spangle, and it was burned as black as a coal.'

His voice sort of cracks at the final sentence, but he gets it out.

Then he forgets how to speak for several minutes –maybe he'll never talk again. What could anyone say after that? What else could be heart while these words hang in the air?

Just as things were going so nicely for them, one of the little boys snatched up the tin soldier and threw him into the stove, he thinks.

The tin soldier stood there dressed in flames.

He remembers the first match that Astra struck, that night she saved their lives.

He can still smell the scent of the burnt wood, almost see the sparks flying from the heater to the carpet, landing next to her hair, singeing his boots.

He thinks of how he's no idea what he's doing, what he's supposed to do, what he will do.

He thinks of how there's a huge bear somewhere out there, waiting like a silent protector, like an unexpected friend, waiting to be needed, and a whole −even bigger- Planet, a ticking bomb.

He thinks of how he has no idea where the next day will find him −alive or dead, sane or mad. He has no idea where the next hour will find him, let alone the next morning.

He thinks of his School, of Karim, of the phantom that used to be the Clockmaster, somewhere in the background, invisible, maybe watching him his entire life. He thinks of the laws of the Chairman, wondering if there are any left for him to break.

He thinks of where he used to be and what he has become.

And all the time, while he's thinking, the words are stuck in his head, repeating themselves like a mantra, like an oath.

Dressed in flames.

Dressed in flames.

The tin soldier, dressed in flames.

t w e n t y - t h r e e

m a t c h   g i r l

She wishes she could read the words herself, see the letters and get their meaning without having someone read them aloud to her, but right now she couldn't do that even if she knew how to read.

Her eyes are full of that damn water again.

How in mars to do that?

How to be that?

On earth.

She, too, was steadfast.

ONCE THE STORY is finished they don't talk for hours —or maybe they're just minutes, but they feel like hours. Then,

"There's something hand-written on the last page," Felix says leaning down, his eyebrows knitted together. 'To put aside for Felix,' he reads. 'About love and sacrifice and being steadfast. About adversity. Add in directions about where to find Christopher Steadfast compartment, after I create it.' He takes in a deep breath, and turns the book over. "It's really tiny, I can't see very well... 'Thirty-fourth compartment to the right, after the Clock'. Astra, do you think...?"

The chair is empty.

Astra's footsteps are already thudding down the hall.

Felix flings the book down and jogs after her.

END OF PART 1

Liked it?

Don't forget to review!

Did you know how much a single positive review can help an author out?

If a book has over a certain number of reviews it's automatically bumped up to the retailer's bestseller list!

So just write a few words to show your appreciation for the author's hard work!

The creation of this book would not have been possible without the help of the amazing **tumblr** community. I went to you guys for support and encouragement, and found inspiration. When you said that I wasn't ruined I believed you -that says it all. I love you and I need you. Thank you so much for following and supporting my blog, **writer**, via **@litlereddoll**. I still don't get why you do it, but thank you.

Not only this book, but also its author wouldn't be here if it wasn't for someone *—my* someone. You are my constant source of strength and happiness. You know who you are to me and why everything I ever write will be dedicated to you.

M.C. FRANK has been living in a world of stories ever since she can remember. She started writing them down when she could no longer stand the characters in her head screaming at her to give them life.

Recently she got her university degree in physics and is now free to pursue her love of reading and writing, as well as her free-lance job of editor-in-chief. She currently lives with her husband in a home filled with candles, laptops and notebooks, where she rearranges her overflowing bookshelves every time she feels stressed.

She loves to connect with her readers and keeps sending them her books for free, but that's ok. She's found the most amazing friends and readers on **tumblr**, and they are what keeps her going when things get rough.

Connect with her on social media for awesome and regular giveaways and free copies of her books! She would also love to talk to you about anything writing or publishing related.

Blog: **bookshelfstories.blogspot.com**

Twitter: **@mcfrank_author**

Instagram: **mcfrank_author**

Tumblr: **@litlereddoll**

Facebook Page: **M.C. Frank**

Goodreads: **M.C. Frank**

Youtube: **M.C. Frank**

Swoon Reads: **M.C. Frank**

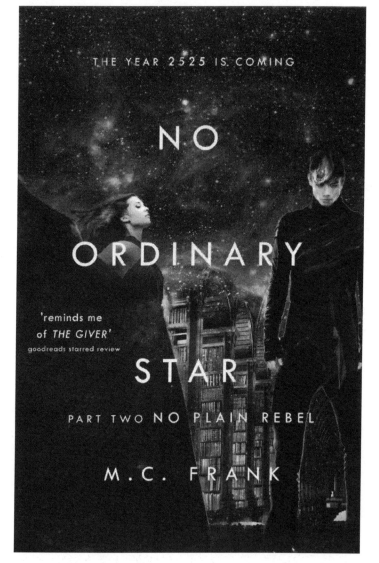

THE YEAR 2525 IS COMING

NO

ORDINARY

'reminds me
of *THE GIVER*'
goodreads starred review

STAR

PART TWO NO PLAIN REBEL

M.C. FRANK

sink your teeth into
your favorite story and
discover new ones
to swoon over

NEW DELUXE
BOOK CANDY
CLASSICS

look for them wherever books are sold!

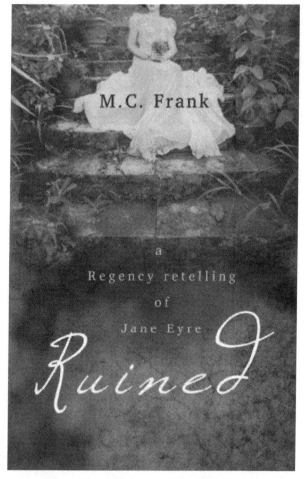

30437100R00100

Made in the USA
Columbia, SC
27 October 2018